D0915114

SECRETS OF THE CASTLETON MANOR LIBRARY™

Tell No Tales

Marlene Chase

Annie's®
AnniesFiction.com

Books in the Secrets of the Castleton Manor Library series

Library of Congress-in-Publication Data
Tell No Tales / by Marlene Chase
p. cm.
I. Title
        2018942464

AnniesFiction.com
(800) 282-6643
Secrets of the Castleton Manor Library™
Series Creator: Shari Lohner
Series Editor: Lorie Jones
Cover Illustrator: Jesse Reisch

10 11 12 13 14 | Printed in China | 9 8 7 6 5 4 3

Faith Newberry pulled into a parking spot outside Snickerdoodles Bakery & Tea Shop.

She glanced at the big display window framed with twinkling lights and smiled. The festive display featured colorful pastries atop fluted plates. There were cakes with pink icing and delicate green holly, plum and mince pies, and mile-high cupcakes with festive sprinkles. Cookies in holiday tins twirled on revolving stands.

"It looks like they've started prepping early for the Christmas Walk," she said to Watson, her handsome black-and-white tuxedo cat. On Sunday, all the downtown businesses would be welcoming shoppers with special sales and refreshments.

Watson rose up on his back legs and braced his front paws against the SUV window, staring in the direction of Happy Tails Gourmet Bakery, which supplied tunaroons, his favorite snack.

Faith's good friend Midge Foster owned the bakery. She was also a first-class veterinarian.

"Don't worry, Rumpy," she told her pet fondly. "I won't forget your tunaroons."

The cat twitched his ears in annoyance and jumped into the back window.

He had earned the nickname Rumpy after losing part of his tail in an accident as a kitten. Clearly, Watson thought the appellation was quite beneath his dignity. But he usually forgave Faith—particularly when it was time for dinner. They'd been together through thick and thin since the day she'd rescued him from the freezing, wet snow as he hid in terror behind a Dumpster.

Faith and her aunt Eileen had agreed to meet at Snickerdoodles, but she was a few minutes early. Eileen Piper was the head librarian at Candle House, a privately funded library near the bakery. The two had always shared a love of books, but the bond between them had grown deeper since Faith moved to Lighthouse Bay to take up duties as a librarian herself at Castleton Manor.

Faith loved working at the pet-friendly mansion retreat for booklovers. Today another group of guests—children's authors and illustrators—would arrive to enjoy its amenities.

For the last several weeks, Faith had been researching and arranging displays of classic books for the event jointly sponsored by the Candle House Library. It meant she'd get to work with her aunt for an afternoon of storytelling featuring the projects of the manor's guests.

She leaned back in the warmth of her idling SUV to watch for Eileen. She could hear strains of Christmas carols echoing from a shop across the street. The town was a fairyland. The snow appeared crisp and even, and in the distance, the bay shone cobalt blue. The lovely old lighthouse stood tall and proud against a backdrop of clear blue sky. Shoppers browsed along tastefully decorated streets, peering through inviting display windows at the goodies inside the warm shops.

Faith glanced idly through the rearview window to see a long, black car approaching and taking the empty parking space behind her.

At the wheel was a large, burly man with a thick, black beard and goggle-like glasses with heavy rims. Next to him was a woman with pale hair, wearing a blue scarf.

But what was that? She squinted. A parrot perched on the man's shoulder.

Some people have unusual tastes in pets, she mused, remembering the literary agent who had brought a ferret to a retreat at the manor.

A low growl came from the back window where Watson lay—or rather prowled, head bent low in the confined space. He'd obviously spied a member of the animal kingdom, and it wasn't one he expected to get along with.

Suddenly Faith was thrust forward against the steering wheel. She whipped her head around and gaped in astonishment. The bearded man had bumped into them!

Watson gave a frantic yowl. He arched his back and puffed up, hissing.

The bird's red-and-green wings frantically beat against the windshield of the car behind them.

The bearded man mouthed something and batted at the fluttering wings as he quickly backed away from Faith's bumper.

The parrot hopped onto the man's head and clung there, opening and closing its beak in soundless fury, while the pale-haired woman in the passenger seat clapped her hand over her mouth.

Shocked, Faith jumped out of her vehicle to assess the damage.

The man lumbered out of his car. Before slamming the door, he flapped his hands at the bird to keep the creature inside.

At the same moment, Eileen stepped out of the Candle House Library and rushed toward them, her features wreathed in confusion.

Faith checked her car but didn't notice any damage except for a tiny scratch or two on the bumper. But she was the one with a right to be angry. She'd been legally parked, and he had rammed his car into hers—not the other way around.

"That nasty feline," the man groused, yanking his navy peacoat over his barrel chest. "Teasing old Harley like that—leering at him through the window like he was going to swallow him whole. That's what caused this whole mess."

Faith opened her mouth to object, but she was too stunned for words. Who was this person? How could he accuse her cat of causing him to run into her?

The man bent down to inspect the damage—first to his car and then to hers. Straightening up, he waved a hand as though shooing away a bothersome fly. "No harm done. You can thank your lucky stars." He had an accent she couldn't quite identify.

Faith was still too stunned to speak. She studied him for a moment before glancing at the passengers in his car.

The parrot continued to flap its wings and fly at the glass while the woman inside raised her arms to protect herself against the whirling maelstrom.

The woman struggled to get out of the vehicle without letting the bird out, then ran toward them on high heels, her blonde hair flying over her long blue coat. "Herbie!" she shouted, tugging at the man's coat sleeve. "*Bitte*. You are making a scene."

"Stay out of this," he told the woman.

She glanced at the small group of onlookers milling around on the sidewalk, then stared down at her feet and wrapped her arms around her slender frame. Her cheeks glowed red with embarrassment. "Let us go now," she whispered.

"Get back in there with Harley." His scowl was worthy of the scariest pirate straight out of *Treasure Island*.

The woman teetered on her high heels, then turned away. But not before Faith saw the glitter of contempt in her eyes.

"What exactly is going on here?" Eileen planted herself between Faith and Black Bart and crossed her arms. Her eyes resembled blue shards of ice.

The man took a step back, visibly affected by the small woman. "It's nothing, ma'am. There's barely a scratch on her car. No harm done to the damsel." He grimaced. "That cat in the window made me lose me moorings for a bit."

"Me moorings"? Why is he talking like a pirate?

"I'm calling the police." Eileen whipped out her cell phone.

"No, wait," Faith broke in. "There doesn't seem to be any real damage to my car."

Eileen turned to Faith. "Are you sure?"

"We should let it go," Faith said with a pleading look at Eileen. Everyone was okay, and after all, it was Christmas.

"We'll be on our way then," the man announced. Without an apology or another word, he returned to his car.

The lady slid in on the passenger side. She held her hands in front of her face as though to ward off the noxious parrot.

But the bird quickly settled on the man's shoulder, squawking and bobbing its ruffled ruby head.

"Let's get in your car," Eileen ordered, taking Faith by the arm. "Until the gawkers leave."

Inside the vehicle, Watson remained vigilant in the back window, only leaping to the front when the man's car careened around them and disappeared down the street.

Faith swept the cat into her arms, smoothing his ruffled fur. "Settle down," she murmured. "It's all right now."

"I can't believe it. The man bumps into you and blames you for it—and poor Watson." Eileen scratched the cat behind his ears. "They certainly aren't from around here," she added in her best New England accent.

And suddenly Faith felt laughter bubbling up inside her. "Am I losing my marbles, or did that guy look like he just got off a pirate ship? Though I've never heard of a pirate named Herbie."

"Or a parrot named Harley," Eileen said. "I couldn't tell, but did you happen to see if the man had a peg leg?"

They broke into uproarious laughter as Watson glared at them. After a few moments, he hopped into the back seat and lay down on the plaid blanket.

Faith cleared her throat. "Are you still up for coffee?"

"Since we're here, why not? Besides, there are a few things I want to go over with you for the story reading." Eileen climbed out of the SUV, settling her red tam atop her shoulder-length brown hair.

Faith promised Watson they wouldn't be long and followed Eileen inside.

At the counter, Faith placed her order. "Dark roast, please." She turned to her aunt. "I really need a pick-me-up."

"I'll have the same," Eileen said.

When they received their coffees, they carried them to a table near the back.

"You sure you're all right, honey?" Eileen asked, reaching across the table with one knobby hand.

Faith pressed it gently, careful of her aunt's rheumatoid arthritis, which she knew was especially painful in cold weather. But Eileen was not one to let something like arthritis hold her back. In addition to her duties as librarian at Candle House, she was active in the town's garden club, which helped to keep up the Victorian garden at Castleton, and she was an avid knitter. "I'm fine," she told her. "Though a bit rattled."

"And who wouldn't be? We get a lot of tourists this time of year, but most of them have a little respect for the locals. The nerve of that man." Eileen sipped her coffee and let out a long, appreciative sigh. "How are plans for the children's authors and illustrators conference shaping up?"

"It's hard to believe it's here already," Faith said. "The welcome banquet is tonight. Marlene's in a dither, of course."

Marlene Russell was the assistant manager of Castleton Manor. Her sometimes prickly disposition made her difficult to work with at times, but she could always be counted on to dot every i and cross every t.

Eileen raised her brows. "What is she upset about now?"

"She came by the cottage last night to make sure I had the classics display ready. And she wanted to confirm that I had included her favorites—*My Friend Flicka* and *The Adventures of Pippi Longstocking*."

"Do you suppose she used to be a drill sergeant before she started working at the manor?" Eileen joked.

Faith laughed.

"And we all know your Mr. Jaxon has great regard for her organizational abilities." She gave Faith a sly wink.

Faith frowned. "Wolfe's not *my* Mr. Jaxon."

Wolfe was co-owner of Castleton Manor and an international business magnate, as well as a warmhearted person who attracted people wherever he went. He was probably the most sought-after bachelor in Lighthouse Bay. Since she'd accepted the position of librarian at the manor, they had become friends. Just friends.

"I think he has an eye for you," Eileen said, her eyes sparkling. "Protest if you must."

Faith laughed. "You're impossible, but I love you anyway."

Her aunt put her cup down with a firm *clink*. "Now refresh my memory. The reading for the children is scheduled for Saturday afternoon. Is that right?"

"Yes. We'll be ready for them. I understand a bus will be bringing them to Castleton."

"And the weatherman has promised to cooperate." Eileen smiled. "Though if we should have snow, it will be even more delightful for the sleigh ride through the grounds. Some of these kids have few opportunities to enjoy such lovely accommodations."

Faith knew her aunt found joy in reading to children, especially underprivileged or homeless ones. Eileen had worked with the school system to identify the children who would get the most enjoyment out of a trip to the manor. It saddened Faith to know that even in Lighthouse Bay there were children who moved from one temporary home to another—or worse, who had no home at all.

"Brooke is planning a feast the children won't be able to resist," Faith said. Brooke Milner was the newly promoted head chef at the manor. She was one of Faith's dearest friends and a fellow member of the Candle House Book Club, which also included Eileen and Midge. "Gourmet ground round burgers and oven-baked fries."

"What about dessert? I suppose it's too cold for ice cream," Eileen said with a pout.

Faith grinned. "It's never too cold for ice cream. Sundaes with their choice of toppings, complete with whipped cream and a cherry.

And speaking of ice, I'd better get back. I don't want to leave Watson in the car too long. He's had a particularly trying afternoon."

They walked outside together, breathing in the crisp air.

Eileen linked her arm through Faith's. "People who visit Cape Cod only in the summer don't know what they're missing."

"Have you ever seen the bay look more beautiful than it does right now?" Faith rested her hand on the driver's side door and gazed at the white-and-blue landscape.

Waves frothed as they rolled leisurely to the pale shore. Clouds scudded across the powder-blue sky. Faith felt her shoulders relax and her breathing slow.

"I never tire of the view," Eileen said, as if reading her mind.

"Hey, Mrs. Piper." A boy of nine or ten approached, grinning at Eileen. He wore jeans and a brown cloth jacket with no scarf or hat, and his soiled tennis shoes were laced only partway on his feet. A swatch of dark hair fell over his left eye. He held a battered hockey stick.

"Hello, Kevin." Eileen smiled at him. "Where are you off to this afternoon?"

"I'm going to the library. My teacher said to pick a book about a sport we like. You think there'll be some books about hockey?"

"There are lots of them," Eileen answered. "You'll be surprised. I saw one just the other day about a boy who makes his own hockey sticks."

Kevin suddenly spied Watson, whose nose was pressed against the window of the SUV. He placed his hands on the glass to peer excitedly into Watson's green eyes.

"That's my cat, Watson. Do you want to pet him?" Faith opened the door.

Watson leaped into her arms, though his focus was fixed on Happy Tails.

She leaned toward Kevin so the boy could pet the cat. Watson purred. "I see he likes you," she told him, touched by the boy's gentle demeanor.

"I like him too," he said, withdrawing his hand from Watson's head. "What happened to his tail?"

"He lost part of it in an accident when he was a kitten," Faith explained. "But it doesn't stop him from getting around."

The boy nodded and thrust his hands into his pockets. "I wish I had a cat. Or a dog. But Mom says we can't have one of them in our apartment." He shrugged. "Well, I gotta go. Bye."

"A sweet boy," Eileen remarked as Kevin walked away. "I wish all the kids who visit the library were as polite."

"Good manners say a lot about his parents," Faith said.

"In Kevin's case, there's just one parent," Eileen replied. "His mother is raising him alone. I'm not sure how she does it. She usually brings him to the library, and she seems quite protective of him. She's probably in her early thirties, moved here from upstate New York. She's a nice woman, but she doesn't say much. I think she has a hard time making ends meet."

Faith watched the slump of the boy's retreating shoulders. He kicked at a stone in the timeworn way of all boys, and the sight of it made Faith strangely sad. "Will he be at the reading and sleigh ride?"

"I'm pretty sure he will," Eileen said.

After chatting about the children's event for a few more minutes, Faith sighed. "I'd better go. Marlene has summoned me to greet the guests tonight, and there's to be mingling prior to the banquet. No rest for the weary."

"Have a good time. I'll talk to you soon." Eileen waved goodbye as she walked to the library.

Faith climbed into her SUV, started the ignition, and pulled away from the curb. She was about to turn the corner to head back to the manor when she noticed the long, black car that had bumped her.

Across the street, the bearded man sat behind the wheel of his idling car, the parrot still perched on his shoulder. His gaze seemed fixed on Kevin, who had left the library and was ambling down the street. The boy now carried a book in addition to his hockey stick.

Faith stared. She and Eileen had watched the man drive away with the parrot and the woman with the German accent after he'd rammed her bumper. Surely, after drawing a crowd and being thoroughly rebuffed by an angry Eileen, the rude man would not want to hang around.

What was he doing back here? And why did he appear to be watching Kevin so intently?

"There's no accounting for some people," she said to Watson.

Feeling a sudden shiver, Faith pressed the accelerator firmly, eager to leave unfriendly tourists behind and get back to the warmth of Castleton Manor.

Faith took the shoveled path from her cottage to the manor with Watson prancing along behind.

The cat had insisted on scooting through the cottage door after her. Obviously, he was not about to be left at home after his demanding encounter with an irksome parrot.

"You'll have to wait in the library until after dinner," she told him.

He refused to respond to that.

The crisp air and serene landscape refreshed her spirit as she walked. The historic Victorian garden wore its best vestments, snow lending sugarcoated enchantment to every tree and bush.

Ahead lay the French Renaissance château-style mansion. It was bathed in shimmering light that defined its impressive turrets and balconies, its alcoves and many windows. The velvety darkness provided a splendid backdrop for the manor with its grand halls, parlors, fireplaces, and elegant bedrooms. A great hall was paved with marble and led through French doors to the loggia, which afforded spectacular views of the ocean.

"Can you believe we get to work here every day?" she asked Watson.

But the cat seemed much more interested in nosing along the walkway to see what treasures might linger there.

"Check out those statues and topiaries," she chatted on, intrigued by the snow and ice that clung to their ridges and spheres. Above them, giant firs stretched toward a star-bejeweled sky.

Faith's thoughts drifted to the upcoming retreat. It should be an exciting event, although there would be a competitive edge. Writers would read their manuscripts to the delight of children but also to attract the interest of the publishing representative who would be listening as well. Not to be left out, illustrators had been invited to exhibit their portfolios.

She looked forward to getting a peek inside the world of children's literature, and she was pleased that Wolfe would be able to participate in the retreat as well as in other local fund-raisers and special activities during the holidays.

Wolfe traveled often, but this year he would be home for the Christmas season. The whole Jaxon family—Wolfe's widowed mother, Charlotte, and his younger brothers, Richard and Blake, along with Richard's wife and three children—would soon gather at the manor.

Faith scooped up Watson in her arms as she neared the door. She wasn't about to chase him through the manor. She planned to leave her pet in the library until the banquet was over.

She hesitated at the incredible Great Hall Gallery. Like everyone who saw it, she found the room breathtaking, and she especially loved the marble statue of Dame Agatha Christie with pen in hand. It was particularly stunning in early evening.

But there was no time now to enjoy the room's elegant ambience. She needed to greet the new guests.

The cat squirmed in his human's arms, but she held him tight.

Rats! He wouldn't be able to explore all the manor's nooks and crannies tonight.

He loved sinking his claws into the velvety soft carpet on the staircase and pawing the tall green palms that rose to the high ceiling in shiny plant stands. The stone figures that resembled humans made excellent hiding places from which to launch himself onto the cool marble floor. And he was especially fond of slipping through the doors at the far end of the room—the doors that led out onto a platform where he might peer through the railing to the ocean.

His person turned away.

Double rats! She was going to take him straight to the library. At least it was an interesting room too. There were cubbyholes to explore and comfortable chairs to curl up in by the fire. There would be cool water and sometimes a delicious treat in his bowl.

His human was kind to him, so the cat supposed he should be good, even if he didn't like being carried. He much preferred to choose his destinations and get there by his own power.

But what was that? The cat heard a sound coming from one of the doors that led out to the balcony. He squirmed in his person's arms and strained to listen. He heard human voices, and one of them was familiar—disagreeably familiar.

Gathering all his strength, the cat wriggled free and streaked across the marble floor before he could be scooped up again.

"Rumpy?" As his human chased him, she called him by that silly name he disliked so much.

The cat kept going. The voice he didn't like grew louder, and he smelled something. He stopped for a moment and sniffed. It reminded him of that big squawking bird he'd seen that afternoon.

He realized one of the voices belonged to the nasty human who had hit their car and sent him sprawling.

But the cat would protect his person this time. He wouldn't let that bearded human near her again. He hissed fiercely.

"Rumpy!" his human called, still pursuing him.

Then he felt himself snatched up and held fast in human clutches once again.

Faith gripped Watson and snuck behind the statue of Agatha Christie. "Hush," she whispered.

He quieted, but his ears lay flat against his head.

Two men stood near the French doors leading to the loggia, their voices penetrating the stillness in the Great Hall Gallery. What were they doing out here instead of in the banquet hall with the other guests? No doubt they were latecomers, but she was arrested by an angry voice that carried through the room.

"There weren't enough conferences in New York?" one of the men snapped. "You had to come clear out here to the Cape."

"It's a free country, me hearty," a deep voice replied.

The odd, otherworldly vocabulary fell on Faith's ears with startling recollection. It was the voice of the black-bearded man who had bumped into her car that afternoon.

She peeked around the statue of Agatha Christie. It *was* him. The man was no random tourist of Lighthouse Bay. He was a guest of the retreat.

The man wore a black suit jacket and a bow tie, and the flashy parrot was perched on his shoulder. The bird emitted a shriek that was likely to send every seagull within a one-mile radius winging to safety.

Are you kidding me? Faith thought wildly. *Is he really going to take that bird to the banquet?*

Guests of the manor were invited to bring their pets but not when the animals infringed on the peace and well-being of other guests. She had a feeling this parrot would definitely disturb some of the other visitors.

"You're a real piece of work. I know why you're really here." The other man was slender and half the size of his bearded companion. He had thinning blond hair and a sparse mustache below an aquiline nose. There was something clean and appealing in his youthful face.

The bearded man strode a few steps away, then spun around on his bootheel. The parrot wobbled unsteadily but held on. "I have my reasons for being here, and they have nothing to do with a washed-up writer who should have walked the plank a long time ago."

The blond man scoffed.

"I have better things to do with my art than waste it on your anemic stories," the bearded man continued. "I'm finished with the series. And finished with you, partner. I'm finding a new writer for my characters. And I'm turning over a new leaf." Then he laughed uproariously, repeating the phrase.

"You've made your point, Grissom." The blond man's voice rose to a high, implacable tenor. "But stay out of my way if you know what's good for you."

The bearded man strode back over to the other man and shook a finger in his face. "You'll get nowhere with your pathetic Perry and the Pirate series now. It was my drawings that sold 'em, but I'm going for the real booty. You'll flounder in your own wretched stew."

Faith's head spun with sudden recognition. A couple of years earlier, the Perry and the Pirate series—written by Felix Anderson with illustrations by Herbert Grissom—had been immensely popular and serious contenders for prestigious awards.

She took a quick breath and held it. Here they were, the two of them. How strange that this small, mild-mannered man was the writer of those swashbuckling tales of a brave young boy protecting his treasure from a greedy pirate. A pirate so perfectly personified in the illustrator standing next to him.

"When the sun sets, you'll be going down in the briny," Herbert spat, poking his finger into Felix's chest.

Felix brushed aside the intrusive hand and smoothed the lapels of his white dinner jacket. "You can't help yourself, can you?" he snarled. "Still dressing and acting like the blackhearted thief you are. Stay away from me." He turned and stomped away, his steps echoing on the marble floor.

"Awk! New leaf!" the parrot screeched as Herbert left the room as well, shaking his head and scowling at Felix's retreating back.

Faith crouched lower against the statue and waited until both men had disappeared.

So, they had once been partners, but the illustrator was firing the writer. Had Herbert come to this retreat—outside of his usual working zone—to rub Felix's nose in the dismissal? Herbert had said, *I have my reasons*. What were they? Why had he come?

Holding Watson in a firm grip, she slipped through a side door and headed toward the library. It would be nice to lock herself in with the cat for a quiet evening among the shelves of books, but she was expected at the welcome banquet.

And she and Herbert Grissom were sure to cross paths again soon anyway.

After leaving Watson curled up in one of the chairs in the library, Faith made her way to the banquet hall.

Retreat guests were gathering and chatting amiably, fluted punch glasses in hand. Some admired the stately alabaster columns, the great chandeliers, and the massive fireplace with three openings in the hearth.

At a nearby table she spotted Herbert Grissom—fortunately sans parrot—seating himself and the tall blonde woman who had been in the car with him that afternoon.

The woman was dressed in a red blouse and sleek black trousers. She wore a cream scarf, and her blonde hair was swirled in a pretzel-like braid atop her head. With her pale-blue eyes, she resembled a grown-up Gretel. Faith could almost imagine her holding hands with a freckle-faced Hansel and tossing crumbs along the path to a gingerbread house.

Faith scanned the room and noticed Wolfe beckoning to her. She hurried toward him, aware of Herbert watching her. When she glanced at him, she saw him furrow his brow. He obviously recognized her.

"I saved a place for you," Wolfe said as he pulled out a chair for her. His light-gray dinner jacket accentuated the silver hair at his temples, and his blue bow tie drew out his piercing eyes.

"Thank you," Faith said as she sat down. She was relieved to be away from the scrutiny of the bullying artist. "I'm sorry I'm a bit later than I planned." She started to say she'd been interrupted by a less-than-amiable guest but held back.

"It's fine." Wolfe took his seat on her right. "We haven't started yet."

Faith regarded the elegant table set with the best china and the finest crystal glasses. At each place setting were two linen napkins—one crimson, one white—bound into holly-etched silver rings. She turned to Marlene who sat on her other side. "Everything looks beautiful."

Marlene gave her a satisfied smile, then stood to command the attention of the guests. Her manner was calm and collected as she welcomed the guests and gave a few brief announcements.

Then the servers bustled inside the banquet hall and served the amazing dinner, consisting of tender roast beef with rich gravy, twice-baked potatoes, and sautéed asparagus.

"Marlene tells me you and Eileen have made some interesting plans for the authors and illustrators," Wolfe said to Faith. "And I'm excited about the children coming to the manor. They'll brighten up the place." He gave her a conspiratorial wink.

"Yes. Lunch, a sleigh ride, and story time around the fire. Eileen has been working hard to make the necessary arrangements." Faith smiled. "It's wonderful of you to open the mansion up to them. I think it'll be a day they'll never forget."

"We'll all do our best to make sure it is," Wolfe said.

An elderly woman with tight gray curls addressed Marlene. "When is Mr. Delacroix expected, may I ask?"

"He's scheduled to arrive on Wednesday," Marlene answered. "He'll be here in plenty of time for the manuscript readings."

Faith had learned that Léon Delacroix represented Maple Publishing in Canada, and the company planned to open a subsidiary line in New York. He had expressed a sensitivity to the work of new writers and illustrators and had graciously offered his services for this retreat. Cape Cod's proximity to New York and his willingness to donate his fee for the benefit of needy children in the area had made him an attractive choice.

"I understand he's French. Well, of course with a name like Delacroix he must be," the woman continued.

"French Canadian," Faith said.

Eager brown eyes sparkled in her small, round face. "I can't wait to meet him, especially since my manuscript is about a mouse born in the Bastille—a very special mouse, you understand. He was most influential in helping the revolutionaries in 1789."

Marlene gave the woman a professional smile. "How charming," she said.

A young woman wearing a chic evening dress reddened slightly. She exchanged a glance with a middle-aged man with heavy eyebrows who sat next to her.

Faith cringed. They probably assumed the elderly woman and her mouse story were eccentric and judged her a novice in the field of writing. But Faith knew that appearances could be deceiving. The guests of the retreat came from varying backgrounds—some with published credentials and others eager to learn and advance in their chosen craft.

The guests launched a discussion of their potential manuscripts and illustrations. Excitement rode high, and everyone seemed to be in a jovial mood when dessert was served.

Brooke has outdone herself, Faith thought as she tucked her spoon into an individual apple tart with a toasty walnut crust. The apples atop the tart had been cut to form a rose—the pale fruit rimmed with a thin touch of the red peel. The filling was a rich maple custard, smooth and sweet.

"Three cheers for the chef," someone called out.

Faith caught Brooke's eye where she was standing in the doorway, monitoring the guests' reactions.

As the chef, trained at the prestigious Le Cordon Bleu College of Culinary Arts in Boston, Brooke was in charge of developing the menu at Castleton Manor. She received high accolades for her culinary creations, and, in Faith's opinion, she deserved every one of them.

Brooke disappeared for a moment, then reappeared with a petite woman in tow. The woman's dark, curly hair was drawn back from her round, blushing face. Her eyes were large, thickly fringed, and the color of maple syrup.

Faith had never seen the woman before. Then she recalled that Brooke had hired some temporary kitchen staff for the busy wChristmas season at the manor, so the woman was probably one of Brooke's new helpers.

"Ladies and gentlemen," Brooke announced, smiling broadly, "this is the baker who came up with today's dessert. Let's hear it for Angelina."

Applause echoed in the banquet hall.

The dark-haired woman seemed embarrassed, but she gave a tiny bow.

Brooke gently nudged the woman a little farther into the elegant room.

Suddenly the woman stopped and froze. Her face became ashen, and her knees seemed to buckle.

Brooke appeared concerned and quickly whisked Angelina away, closing the door behind them.

As the applause died down and the guests returned to their desserts, Faith wondered if she was the only one who had seen the woman nearly collapse.

Was she ill? Or had she seen something that shocked or frightened her?

3

From her cottage window, Faith gazed out on the manor's snow-covered gardens fringed by frosted evergreens. The old Christmas carol echoed in her mind:

> *Good King Wenceslas looked out*
> *On the feast of Stephen*
> *When the snow lay round about*
> *Deep and crisp and even.*

The tranquility of the scene contrasted sharply with yesterday's restless activity, ruffled tempers, and later the merriment of the welcome dinner.

She stroked Watson, who was perched on the back of the couch. He peered intensely through the glass. "Fabulous, isn't it, Rumpy?"

He swiveled around to meet her glance through eyes narrowed into slits. He hopped down abruptly and trotted off into the kitchen. If he'd had more than a stump of a tail, it would have been held straight up like a flagpole in a sign of protest.

"Aren't we sensitive this morning?" she murmured with a grin. Who said cats couldn't understand words? To make up for her use of the nickname, she added a treat to his usual breakfast kibble.

The noisy parrot had riled the cat, and to be truthful, the bird's owner had caused considerable distress for her too. She wondered how the pompous Herbert Grissom would behave today. Perhaps he would be too busy preparing his portfolio for the artists' display to get into trouble. And if the saints were smiling, Harley would be suitably locked up in his cage.

After breakfast, she dressed and made her way to the manor with Watson. As they walked, she considered the upcoming portfolio exhibition.

The writers and illustrators would make good use of the library throughout the retreat, but most questions would pertain to the portfolio exhibition, which would be held in the Great Hall Gallery right outside the library.

As the liaison for the exhibition, Faith had planned it carefully, placing the tables at appropriate intervals and assigning them to the guests who would show their work. The guidelines were succinct and clear—at least she hoped they were—but there were always last-minute concerns to address.

The authors and artists had been invited to display their portfolios in a specified size, along with promotional postcards and feedback cards if desired. Only one portfolio was allowed per guest, and the suggested length of the portfolio was twelve to fifteen pages. A mock-up book could be securely attached to the portfolio. She was excited to see the work of the manor's guests.

Faith and Watson entered the manor and made their way to the walnut-paneled, two-story library where she spent so much of her time.

It was perhaps the most impressive room in the mansion—particularly to the guests attending literary retreats. They loved its floor-to-ceiling shelves of books, the locked glass cases holding rare volumes, the inviting fireplace, and the tasteful chairs and couches where one could read and absorb the world's literature in luxurious comfort.

In honor of the season, the manor staff had installed lighted evergreen garland in graceful scallops along the upper railing. A spectacular Christmas tree with tiny lights and silver balls rose to the ceiling. It was strategically located in a corner between the fireplace and a cluster of red velvet chairs so guests could enjoy it without feeling a sense of dominance or clutter. It came to life with a flip of a switch, lending a luminous glow to the beautiful walnut paneling.

Though she'd seen the tree several times—even watched as the decorations went up—it still took her breath away.

For his part, Watson exhibited the fascination one might expect, occasionally testing a low-hanging silver ball with one delicate paw.

Faith had immediately made it clear that the tree was off-limits for feline prowling.

"You will behave yourself today, won't you, Watson?" she said as she put her coat away, then sat down at her desk.

Watson gave her an innocent look and began grooming himself.

She spent many happy hours at this magnificent desk. Its sides held a large cameo, carved to resemble the face of a Jaxon family ancestor. The entire piece was solid and ornately decorated, down to its elegant legs. Faith had added pens and pencils, along with a paperweight her father had given her containing a sepia replica of her grandmother's face.

She had just retrieved some office supplies from the antique bombé chest near her desk when guests began to drift into the library.

When the door opened, Faith could hear shuffling and animated conversation in the Great Hall Gallery, where some of the participants had started setting up their exhibits.

The guests wore expressions of wonder as they drank in the atmosphere and gazed around the impressive library. A few browsed the shelves of books, and others studied the display of children's classics and contemporary award winners.

The grandmotherly woman Faith recognized from last night's dinner approached her desk.

Faith recalled that the woman's story was about a mouse that had something to do with the French Revolution. "Good morning." She smiled at the woman. "I'm Faith Newberry, the librarian here."

"Maud Tompkins," the woman replied, shaking Faith's hand enthusiastically. "I'm so excited to be at this conference."

"Is there something I can help you with?" Faith asked.

"Has he come yet?" Maud asked in an almost reverent whisper. Then she pushed her glasses up the bridge of her nose.

Faith couldn't help but think how much the lady with springy curls and small, rounded shoulders resembled a furtive gray mouse. "Who do you mean?" she asked.

"Mr. Delacroix, of course," Maud answered. "Ms. Russell said he would be here tomorrow, but I thought he might have arrived early."

"No, he hasn't. I believe he's still on schedule for tomorrow," Faith answered. "Is there anything I can help you with? Do you need any assistance with your exhibit?"

"It's already in place." Maud clasped her hands together. "I couldn't wait so I started early."

"That's great news," Faith said, amused.

Maud smoothed the ruffled white collar that protruded above her tweed jacket. "It's thrilling. I can't wait for Mr. Delacroix to see my illustrations. I drew the pictures for my story myself. I'm so excited to share my book, *Bailey the Bastille Mouse*."

Her eagerness was contagious. "It sounds delightful," Faith said, meaning it.

Maud suddenly noticed the glowing Christmas tree a few yards away. "Oh my!" she exclaimed and moved toward it with quick steps, a hand over her mouth in barely contained elation.

"It sure is a pretty tree," a voice behind Faith said.

Faith turned to see a man in his late thirties holding a copy of *The Jungle Book* that he'd taken off the classics display. He was stocky with coppery hair. Part of a dragon tattoo was visible beneath the sleeve of his slightly stained corduroy jacket. His face held faint pockmarks. Perhaps they were scars from an adolescent case of acne.

The man smiled, but it didn't quite reach his gray, nearly colorless eyes. He extended his hand. "I'm Rupert Rudyard. But please call me Kip."

Faith shook his hand. "That's an interesting name."

"Ironic, isn't it? My parents had a sense of humor."

"Are you related to the famed author?"

"No. More's the pity. My parents were Irish immigrants working for the American dream. They did all right, I suppose, but they pinched pennies to their graves and didn't have anything to leave to us kids. They called me Kip from the day I was born." He gave a short laugh. "But I have to admit it's better than Rupert."

Faith was intrigued, though something about the man's humorless eyes and gruff manner bothered her. "Faith Newberry," she said. "I'm the librarian here."

"Ah. So you're the one who included my namesake among the great writers of children's classics." Kip raised *The Jungle Book*, revealing more of the dragon tattoo above his wrist.

Faith nodded.

"I'm not much into poetry or animal stories myself," Kip went on. "Sci-fi adventure is more to my taste."

"What brings you to the retreat?" Faith asked.

"I'm a somewhat frustrated illustrator," he admitted.

"Don't give up," Faith encouraged. She wondered if art was a new occupation or a hobby for the man. "Everyone starts somewhere."

"Yes, but who can really compete with the big names who've already made it? Like Herbert Grissom." Kip paused. "Grisly Grissom. Now there's a bloke who knows how to navigate the business and schmooze the right people."

Faith winced at the taste of sour grapes.

Kip returned the book to the display and looked at her as though seeing her for the first time. He raised his eyebrows. "So maybe you're the right people," he said, laughing.

His joke left Faith with a bad taste in her mouth. She turned to her desk, hoping he would take the hint and move on.

"Don't take offense," Kip said breezily. "I meant it as a compliment. Well, I'm going back out now to defend my portfolio—against all enemies, foreign and domestic." He winked and strode away, stuffing his hands into the pockets of his pants.

Maud had finished admiring the Christmas tree and slowed as she walked by Faith's desk. "Don't mind him."

"Do you know Mr. Rudyard?" Faith asked, trying not to sound surprised.

"Yes, I've seen him at this kind of event before. He keeps trying to catch the eye of a publisher, but—" Maud broke off and blushed. "He's not very personable, I'm afraid," she finished quietly.

"He seems to know Mr. Grissom," Faith said, remembering Kip's caustic tone when he mentioned Herbert. *Grisly Grissom.* But most writers and would-be writers of children's books would know the famous illustrator's name.

"Oh, you know, dear," Maud said kindly. "It's hard for some folks to applaud the success of others if they can't seem to succeed themselves."

Faith smiled, liking the elderly lady and ready to end thoughts of both Kip and Herbert. She patted Maud's arm in a sudden rush of warmth. "I look forward to seeing your exhibit."

As Maud left the library, Faith realized that excited voices in the corridor had grown louder. Some sort of commotion was going on, and one voice above all the others brought a sudden sense of dread. Leaving Watson curled up in front of the fire, she hurried after Maud.

Faith stared in disbelief at the glowering figure storming down the corridor.

Herbert was clad in red-and-black striped trousers tucked into tall black boots with silver buckles. He wore a white shirt with billowing sleeves and a black vest belted at his thick waist. Black leather bands laced around his wrists, and a red bandanna was tied across his forehead. Bushy black hair fell to his wide white collar. Faith almost expected to see a patch over one eye, but heavy, dark-rimmed glasses dipped over his prominent nose.

"Some blackguard swiped my portfolio," Herbert accused as he marched into the gathering crowd of retreat guests busily preparing their exhibits. "He'd better be giving it back, or I'll see the lily-livered landlubber in the brig!"

"Awk! Pity!" screamed the parrot perched atop Herbert's shoulder.

"What kind of place is this where some wicked scoundrel rips off a man's goods right from under his nose?" Herbert raised his big arms, revealing a scabbard at his left hip containing a fake cutlass that completed his pirate costume.

Alarmed, Faith began to make her way toward him. Obviously, his over-the-top dress and speech were part of his personal portfolio, which probably featured drawings from the Perry and the Pirate series that had gained considerable prominence a couple of years earlier. But bringing that bird in among the press of guests organizing their exhibits was ridiculous and inappropriate—not to mention against the rules.

"Please, Mr. Grissom," Faith called, weaving through the crowd. "I must ask you to keep your voice down. And your pet—"

"Herbie!" The blonde woman with pretzel-braided hair stumbled along behind Herbert, her mouth open, one arm stretched out in appeal. Her dress flapped like an electric-blue banner as her high heels clattered on the floor.

The man spun around to face her. "And you," he said, neglecting his pirate speak for a moment, "didn't you pack my portfolio like I told you?"

"Of course I did," she sputtered. "You saw when I put it in your valise, *ja*? *Ich verstehe nicht*—"

"Ah, more's the pity that our guests will be deprived of your marvelous art," came a sarcastic reply.

Faith instantly recognized the voice, having heard it only moments ago.

Kip stood with his arms folded across his chest and tsk-tsked.

"Awk! Pity! Turn over!" chanted the parrot, bobbing his brilliant feathers and clutching Herbert's shoulder.

Herbert rubbed a hand over his beard. "Still tryin', aye?" he sneered at Kip. "Ye'll not be makin' it in the art world, mate, seeing as you lack any real talent of your own." He tapped his chest where an inside pocket might have been if he'd been wearing a suit instead of the pirate getup.

Kip's face turned suddenly pale, and he spun on his heel and stalked off.

"What is going on? What is all this ruckus about?" Marlene rounded the corner and made for the group gathered around the belligerent would-be pirate. She pointed at Harley. "And what is that parrot doing here?" Her eyes flared with anger. She turned to Faith as though demanding an accounting of the kerfuffle that she had allowed to take place.

Although Faith agreed with Marlene about the bird, she still found it strange that the assistant manager of a pet-friendly establishment would be so put off by animals.

"There be a thief hereabout!" Herbert thundered. "Some blackguard has nicked me portfolio. But I refuse to be hornswoggled. He won't get away with it."

Wolfe suddenly appeared in the melee. "That will be quite enough." His voice struck the air with quiet force.

Instantly, the astonished titters of the group as well as Herbert's rantings were silenced.

Wolfe strode directly into the artist's personal space, fixing him with a calm stare. "You are a guest in this house, sir, but not the only guest. As for your pet, you know it is welcome here at Castleton. But the rules about where it is allowed are clearly spelled out, and you are in violation of those rules."

"I was just on me way to discharge Harley, my good man," Herbert said, belligerence faltering, his face losing its crimson flush. "But discovering the theft set me fair off me moorings."

"If you'll come with me, we'll discuss your missing portfolio," Wolfe said calmly.

But Herbert made no move to obey. "I demand every room be

searched. It's me blooming livelihood that's been swindled." His voice began to rise again, and he scanned the room. "Where's that scoundrel Anderson? He would love nothing better than to see me ruined."

Faith glanced down the line of tables and spotted Felix Anderson watching intently. Was it possible the discharged writer of the famous team had been responsible for the disappearance of Herbert's work? He had the kind of physique that could easily slip through a door unnoticed, and he had been the target of Herbert's blistering tirade the night before.

"We will sort everything out," Wolfe assured him. "Now please come with me."

Herbert glared at the bystanders before following Wolfe down the corridor.

Harley screeched again as he was carried along on Herbert's shoulder, talons dug in.

Faith knew the bird would be remanded to the "brig" in Herbert's "cabin" or entrusted to the animal caretakers on staff at Castleton. Pets were given the best of accommodations in the manor's kennels when their owners wished to attend an event where the animals were not allowed.

The woman in the blue dress and braided hair slipped to one side and pressed herself against the wall, clearly hoping no one noticed her.

"Please, everyone, continue preparing your wonderful displays," Marlene said authoritatively. Faith might not always get along with the assistant manager, but there was no denying she kept a cool head in a crisis. She appeared completely unruffled by events, and her unflappable manner had calmed upset guests more than once in the past.

The guests complied, but their hushed conversations continued as they returned to what they had been doing before the illustrator's outburst.

The woman with the braided hair stayed still for a few moments, watching silently, then began to back away.

Isn't she going to follow Herbert and make sure he's all right?

"Wait, please," Faith called, closing the gap between them. As she drew closer, she read the name tag on the woman's blue dress: *Katrina Grissom*. She assumed the woman was Herbert's wife.

Katrina was a German name. She had even slipped into German when Herbert badgered her about his materials. She had claimed she didn't understand what could have happened to her husband's portfolio.

"I'm so sorry about all this," Faith said, impulsively reaching for the woman's hand. If anyone needed a friend, this woman did. "I'm Faith Newberry, the librarian. And you are Mrs. Grissom, right?"

"Katrina," the woman said in a voice both apologetic and sullen. She pulled her hand away and stared down at her shoes.

"I hope your husband's materials are recovered quickly so he can participate—"

"You don't need to pretend," Katrina broke in harshly. Something seethed behind those powder-blue eyes, something that could not accept condolence or overture of friendship. "Herbie's temper causes trouble. We should not have come here."

"I'm sure Mr. Jaxon can help with this misunderstanding," Faith said, though she wasn't at all sure, nor did she know quite what to do with Katrina Grissom. "Can I get you something? Coffee or tea?"

Katrina shook her head.

Surely she must be worried about her husband and want to be with him, though the two had shown little camaraderie, let alone affection. "Do you want me to take you to your husband?"

"I will go to my room now," Katrina said abruptly, clutching her handbag and turning away. "Herbie can take care of himself." She walked away, shoulders rigid.

So much for that special holiday feeling, Faith thought as she watched the woman walk down the corridor on wobbly high heels.

4

By afternoon, the retreat was humming along as planned, and if the guests were still nettled by the uproar Herbert had caused, they had the good grace not to speak of it, at least when Faith was within earshot.

Faith spent some time browsing the exhibits during the downtime at the library. She was impressed in particular with Maud's startlingly good drawings in her book, *Bailey the Bastille Mouse*. She was pleased to see the enthusiasm of the other guests who surrounded Maud and praised her work. Maud flushed with pleasure.

Clearly the old maxim "Never judge a book by its cover" applied to Maud. Who would guess the diminutive, never-before-published retired teacher would create a story so winsome and clever?

Faith couldn't wait to see how the children—and of course the visiting publisher—would respond to the tale. What an excellent way to expose them to a little history.

Most of the guests meandered toward the salon for refreshments, and Faith decided to return to the library.

When she reached the door, she spotted Wolfe coming toward her, his step strong and purposeful. He wore the charismatic smile that never failed to move her—the smile that had been nowhere in evidence when he'd so thoroughly cowed the wannabe-pirate illustrator. She wondered how he had handled the formidable Herbert Grissom.

But his expression gave nothing away. "I'm glad I caught up with you," he said. "Do you have a moment?"

"Of course." Faith unlocked the door. "How did it go with a certain guest?"

Wolfe followed her inside. "Mr. Grissom's quite a piece of work, though they say he's an accomplished illustrator—especially for adventure magazines."

Watson got up from his spot in front of the fire and joined them. He rubbed against Wolfe's legs.

Wolfe obligingly leaned down to pet the cat.

"Herbert illustrated the Perry and the Pirate series that was so popular a couple of years ago," she said. "Did you know the writer of those pirate books is here too?"

Wolfe shook his head.

"That's who Herbert accused of stealing his portfolio. His name is Felix Anderson."

"Have you met Mr. Anderson yet?" he asked.

"Not exactly. I inadvertently overheard a conversation between Herbert and Felix just before the welcome dinner last night." Faith recalled the tension in the air, the animosity clearly in evidence. Watson must have sensed something when he led her there—or rather dragged her when she had intended to go straight to the banquet hall.

Wolfe raised his eyebrows. "What did they talk about?"

"They had some sort of disagreement, and Herbert essentially fired Felix. He claims the reason the books sold so well was only because of his illustrations."

"Mr. Grissom appears to have a pretty high opinion of himself, doesn't he?"

She sighed. "And everyone heard Herbert insinuate that his former partner might have stolen his portfolio. Do you suppose he did? Maybe out of spite or payback for dissolving their partnership?"

"I don't know."

"Do you think we should alert the police?" Faith asked.

"I don't believe it's necessary at the moment," Wolfe said thoughtfully, "but it may come to that at some point."

"What happened when you spoke to Herbert?"

"He agreed to return to his room and search through his belongings.

He also hinted that his wife might have left his portfolio at home. He says she's sometimes forgetful—when she isn't being contrary."

"It sounds like there's not a great deal of harmony in the Grissom home." Faith shuddered as she recalled the look of contempt she had seen in Katrina's eyes after her husband had told her to get back in the car when they were parked outside Snickerdoodles.

"I'm afraid you're right."

"I tried to talk to Katrina after you took Herbert away, but she was pretty—well, contrary," Faith remarked. "She said her husband's temper gets them in trouble and they never should have come to the retreat."

"I wonder why he did come," Wolfe said.

"Maybe he's searching for a new partner or publisher," Faith suggested. "Did Herbert say anything else?"

"He apologized for his outburst and for the parrot. There was something kind of tragic about him. A colorful character for sure." Wolfe shook his head. "It's too bad about the pirate series, but he seems to be stuck in the role of a pirate himself."

"Yes, right down to a parrot and a fake cutlass stuck in his belt. Some of the guests wondered if they'd missed Halloween somehow." Faith brushed back a stubborn lock of hair. "So why would he fire his writer partner? It baffles me."

"There's a lot we don't know," Wolfe answered. "But what I do know is that we can't allow his problems—publishing or otherwise—to interrupt the flow of this retreat and the good things that have been planned for the guests and the kids. You and your aunt have worked hard to coordinate everything."

"We met yesterday to go over plans," Faith said, touched by his praise but not wanting to show it. "That's how I ran into Herbert and Katrina—or rather they ran into me."

"What do you mean?" Wolfe asked.

"I was parked outside Snickerdoodles, waiting for Eileen, and he pulled into the spot behind me. But he didn't stop soon enough. He slammed into my car."

"Are you all right?" Wolfe asked, blue eyes filled with concern.

"Yes. I don't have any bruises, and there's just a tiny scratch or two on my car's bumper. Watson and I were shaken up, but there was no harm done." She grinned. "Ironically, that's what he said: 'No harm done to the damsel.' He claimed it was Watson's fault for teasing his parrot through the rear window where Watson was sitting."

"The nerve of the guy. Did you call the police?"

"No. Eileen wanted me to, and I decided to let it go. But I had no idea he was coming to the manor. I was shocked to see him at the welcome dinner." Faith frowned. "He was none too pleased to see me either."

"I'm so sorry," Wolfe said. "He had better behave himself from this point on, or he'll be walking the plank." He grinned. "Sorry. I couldn't resist."

Faith laughed, and the conversation took a more pleasant turn toward the children's day on Saturday.

Presently, he glanced at his watch. "Our public awaits," he announced. "And if the fates are kind, our bombastic friend will have located his portfolio or made arrangements for it to be delivered so we can continue this retreat in relative peace."

"I think it's going to be a lovely event," Faith said. "I've already met some wonderful authors and illustrators, and the Christmas season adds a special dimension." Warmth spread through her. "The manor is beautiful. I've heard so many compliments."

Marlene appeared at the library door and signaled to Wolfe.

"Thanks for all you've done—and will do," Wolfe said to Faith, then left.

As Faith busied herself tidying up her desk, she quietly sang the carol that had been going through her mind since that morning when she'd gazed out upon the snow-covered grounds of the manor: "Good King Wenceslas looked out on the feast of Stephen . . ."

"We're certainly happy this morning."

She wheeled around to see Brooke entering the library, wearing a white chef's coat and black pants.

"Did the master of the house have anything to do with your buoyant mood?" Brooke gave her a mischievous grin, then answered her own question. "Silly me. Of course he did."

"Don't start," Faith said, shaking her head. Brooke liked to tease her about Wolfe, and she claimed he'd been spending more time at the manor ever since Faith had begun working there. "We were simply discussing the debacle over an artist's missing portfolio. Wolfe had to escort him away like an errant schoolboy."

"I thought I heard a commotion, but I've been busy down in the kitchen since dawn. Well, not really dawn, but it seems like it." Brooke swept a short strand of blonde hair from her forehead, then gave Faith a searching look. "Did everything turn out all right with the guest? Are you okay?"

"Oh yes, that is, we can only hope he behaves himself. And I'm fine."

"Well, that's good," Brooke said, sitting down next to Faith's desk. "My feet are killing me. Do you mind if I sit here for a minute or two before I go back to the salt mines?"

"Be my guest." Faith took a seat at her desk.

"What did you think of that apple tart we served at the welcome dinner?" Brooke asked.

"It was delicious," Faith replied.

"I've never tasted a smoother custard, and the apple rose was nothing short of genius," Brooke gushed. "I saw the smiles on our guests' faces and heard them cheer for Angelina."

"Who is Angelina? Is she one of your temporary helpers?"

Brooke nodded. "Angelina Cordova. Thank goodness Marlene agreed to let me hire her. She's such a hard worker, and she's really creative."

"How did you find her?" Faith asked.

"We met at the market. We were both searching for spices and got to talking about paprika and turmeric and ginger and what kind of cinnamon is the best," Brooke explained. "Then I discovered we both like fish, and I told her about Diva and Bling."

Faith smiled. Brooke's angelfish, Diva and Bling, were a cross between pets and personal date advisers. Brooke claimed the angelfish swam in a certain frenzied pattern whenever a loser guy was nearby or even on the phone.

"Angelina's a single parent," Brooke continued, frowning. "And I know she hasn't had it easy. I notice how carefully she checks the prices of things when we shop together, and she's concerned about how she's going to afford the special hockey stick her son, Kevin, wants for Christmas. I always thought a hockey stick was a hockey stick, but I guess not. Anyway—"

"Did you say her son's name is Kevin?" Faith broke in, suddenly making the connection between the boy named Kevin she'd met with Eileen. A boy who loved hockey.

"Kevin, yes. He's ten years old, and he's so cute. He has curly black hair and a crooked little smile."

"I met him yesterday. Eileen knows him. He comes to the library, and she helps him find books about sports. He was nice and polite, and he took a liking to Watson."

"Kevin is a great kid." Brooke smiled. "I'm so glad I could offer Angelina a job here. It's temporary, but it will give her a little extra to help make ends meet for her son." She knitted her eyebrows together, and she grew quiet for a few seconds before saying, "She hasn't come in yet today."

"Why not?" Faith asked.

"She left a message—something about Kevin starting school late. She said she'd come in as soon as she could. She doesn't like to leave him alone."

"When she came out to receive the applause of the guests last night, it seemed like she almost fainted," Faith said. "Is she okay?"

Brooke frowned. "That surprised me too. She just turned white as a sheet and collapsed. After I ushered her downstairs to the kitchen, I helped her to a chair and got her a glass of water."

"What did she say?"

"When I asked her what happened, she said she had felt suddenly ill but that it was nothing. She kept insisting that she was fine. I made her eat something just in case she had low blood sugar. I couldn't remember the last time I'd seen her eat."

Faith nodded. "Low blood sugar and her natural shyness could have made her collapse. What happened then?"

"A few minutes later, she seemed fine," Brooke said. "She got up and bustled around the kitchen as cool as you please."

"Hmm. Strange. I hope she's not really sick."

"Me too," Brooke said, frowning again. "You're right. She is super shy. She must hate crowds. I should have thought of that before I dragged her out in front of everyone. I definitely won't make her go out and take any more bows." She stood. "Well, I need to run. I have a million things to do before the big party for the kids."

"Everyone is so excited about it."

"Are you sure Wolfe is okay with a bunch of kids running through the manor with all its priceless items?"

"It was his idea in the first place," Faith replied, feeling a singular pride. "And he couldn't be more delighted about the prospect."

"What a guy." Brooke winked mischievously. "Maybe Angelina will have arrived by now." And she was off and running.

Faith wondered why Angelina was late to work. Was she telling the truth? Had Kevin really started school later, or was something else going on? It would have to be something awfully important for Angelina to jeopardize the job that she so desperately needed.

She sighed. Who knew what went on in the secret sanctuary of people's minds?

5

Faith jerked awake at the not-so-subtle thump on her left hip.

Watson leaped down from the bed and stared at her.

"What?" She sat up, trying to focus. Sunlight brightened the room even with the shades drawn. She checked the clock. It was later than her usual rising time. She must have slept through her alarm. "A little impatient this morning, are we?" she asked the cat.

Apparently, Watson had been hungry enough to compromise his dignity by pouncing on her as a reminder that he needed breakfast.

She had slept soundly after delivering her lecture on Professor Clement Clarke Moore, who was credited with authorship of the beloved poem "A Visit from St. Nicholas." Celebrated down through the years in various wrappings since it was first published in 1823, the poem still captivated audiences.

> *'Twas the night before Christmas, when all through the house*
> *Not a creature was stirring, not even a mouse . . .*

She had enjoyed sharing Moore's interesting story. A professor of divinity, biblical learning, and Oriental and Greek literature, he had been an eminent scholar and perhaps hoped to be remembered for his erudite works. Moore stated that he wrote "A Visit from St. Nicholas" for his children, but he was reluctant to claim the work because he thought it was frivolous. It wasn't until 1844 that he first acknowledged in print that he was its author.

However, Moore's claims were disputed, with many scholars claiming Major Henry Livingston Jr. was more likely to have penned the piece.

The lecture had rounded out an eventful day. Faith was glad she had prepared well in advance, and when it was over she felt the guests had enjoyed it. There would likely be renewed interest today in the pristine copy of the poem, illustrated by Jessie Willcox Smith and published in 1912 by Houghton Mifflin. Wolfe had paid a tidy sum for the little book and had purchased a special case for its protection and display in the manor's library.

The guests would be eager to see the book—if she ever got out of bed.

"All right, all right," she told the cat, who was now pacing around the bed and loudly expressing his displeasure at the wait. "I'm up."

After she and Watson ate their breakfast, they walked to the manor through a gentle shower of snow. *Will it ever stop?*

It had snowed some part of every day for a week. All the better for an enchanting sleigh ride with the children. But dealing with boots, coats, and scarves and shaking snow from her hair was a time-consuming business.

Watson, who loved to explore, sometimes got himself into a snowdrift taller than he was. And the cat wasn't at all fond of having his paws wiped before entering the manor.

As Faith and Watson approached the library, she was surprised to see Marlene lingering in the corridor.

The exhibits were a continuing source of interest for everyone, but Marlene was a type A, business-first kind of person who seldom lingered anywhere. She had no doubt been up since the crack of dawn, but she looked as though she'd just stepped out of a beauty parlor. She wore small green earrings that matched her emerald-green suit.

"Good morning." Faith wondered if Marlene would comment on her companion. The assistant manager had made a kind of truce with Watson but preferred that Faith keep the cat in her cottage.

But Marlene scarcely gave Watson a passing glance. Her mind was clearly elsewhere. "I was checking the exhibits," she began tentatively, as though embarrassed to be found standing still. "I see the table assigned to Mr. Grissom is still empty. I had hoped his complaint would have been resolved by now." She narrowed her eyes suspiciously at Faith, as though the whole thing were her fault.

"I haven't heard. When I talked to Wolfe yesterday, he said Mr. Grissom had calmed down. He wasn't demanding that every room in the manor be searched, and he admitted that his wife might have forgotten to pack his portfolio. If so, I'm sure he'll arrange for it to be shipped here."

"I certainly hope there won't be any more trouble, but the Grissoms have not made an appearance today. The breakfast service is over, and they have yet to show." Marlene crossed her arms over her chest. "I don't need this kind of aggravation—not with Mr. Delacroix arriving anytime. I expected these tables to be filled and all the exhibits ready."

Marlene's insistence on perfection was both a bane and a blessing. She couldn't expect everything to operate like well-oiled machinery where human beings were concerned. Could she?

Besides, how difficult would it be to simply remove an empty table if Herbert decided not to exhibit his portfolio? As for causing further disturbance, one could only hope he behaved himself. If not, Wolfe could deal with him and invite him to vacate the premises if necessary.

"If I hear anything or see the Grissoms, I'll be sure to let you know," she told Marlene.

The assistant manager nodded, then marched down the hall to whatever duty claimed her attention.

Watson trotted behind her. No doubt he was off to explore his favorite haunts.

She considered calling him back, but she was loath to draw Marlene's attention to him. *You win this round, Rumpy,* she thought, suspecting that had been his plan all along.

As Faith opened the library door and went inside, she ruminated on the Grissoms' last few days. *Things have not gone well for them from the start.*

Herbert had literally run into the Castleton librarian and then discovered his portfolio missing. He had ruffled the feathers of quite a few guests and gotten into a heated argument with his former partner, whom he may or may not have known was attending the same event.

Faith sighed. Perhaps if she had experienced such a beginning, she might have considered skipping breakfast too.

Guests began filing into the grand two-story library with its welcoming ambience.

A tall woman with a spray of freckles across her nose approached Faith. "I loved your lecture last night. It was wonderful, and I couldn't wait to have a look at the 1912 copy of the poem."

Faith had met Patsy O'Neil at the welcome dinner and remembered her for her uncanny resemblance to illustrations of Pippi Longstocking, the heroine of the children's classic. At thirty-plus, however, she didn't wear braids. Her red hair fell straight from a center part to the narrow shoulders of her shirtwaist dress.

"Thank you. If you put on these gloves, I'll be happy to unlock the case and let you read it for yourself," Faith offered.

"That would be great," Patsy said, grinning and revealing a slight gap between her front teeth. "I love Christmas stories for children and especially 'The Night Before Christmas.' I guess it's just about everybody's favorite, isn't it?"

"I believe so," Faith replied. "But I think it deserves to be."

Patsy chuckled. "I love Christmas. I even named my little Pekingese Holly."

"It's great that we can bring our pets here," an older man with a balding pate and a bushy mustache chimed in. The man held out his hand to Faith. "I'm Howard Watkins, and this is Bandit." He gestured to the big labradoodle at his side.

Faith shook his hand. "It's nice to meet both of you."

"Having our pets with us is one of the best things about the retreat," Maud said. She had approached the group without Faith noticing. She smiled at Faith.

"Oh, good morning," Faith said, happy to see the remarkable lady who had everyone raving about her exhibit.

She'd been impressed with how Maud had handled the attention yesterday. The sweet lady had graciously answered questions about her work, welcoming even the most basic beginner queries. But this morning Maud's eyes looked tired. Faith hoped she wasn't overdoing things.

"I wanted to thank you for your lecture last night," Maud said to Faith. "I thoroughly enjoyed it. No matter who really wrote 'A Visit from St. Nicholas,' it's still a gift to all the children of the world—big and small."

"Yes," Faith agreed. "'A Visit from St. Nicholas' comprises arguably the best-known verses ever written by an American, helping to formulate conceptions of Santa Claus from the midnineteenth century to today. Of course, the poem has had a massive impact on the history of Christmas gift giving." Faith hesitated, realizing she was launching into lecture mode again. She smiled apologetically at the three guests. "I beg your pardon. I get a little carried away sometimes. We can all look forward to a dramatic rendition of the poem later in the week."

"How exciting," Patsy said, her eyes shining. "I'll look forward to that for sure."

"Me too," Howard said. Then he and his dog wandered away.

Patsy carefully closed the 1912 copy of the Christmas poem, reverently returned it to its case, and handed the gloves back to Faith. "Thank you. I must get back to my room. I promised Holly a real romp in the snow before I leave for the workshop." She hurried off.

A little knot of worry appeared on Maud's forehead with Patsy's parting comment. She sighed as she gently turned a page of the book she was perusing.

"Is everything all right, Maud?" Faith asked gently.

"Oh, it has been so good to be here, but I'm worried about my little Mouse."

"Mouse?" Had the character in her book become a little too real?

"My Chihuahua," Maud explained. "I named him Mouse long before Bailey the Bastille Mouse was born. I have the loveliest carrier made just for him."

"He sounds adorable. Why are you worried about him?"

Maud frowned. "Mouse weighs only two pounds, so he always shakes a lot and gets the sniffles. But I think he's caught a cold. This morning, he wasn't interested in his breakfast at all."

"Oh, I'm sorry," Faith said. "My good friend Midge Foster is an amazing veterinarian. She has a concierge practice, and she regularly makes house calls to the manor. Would you like her to stop by and check on Mouse?"

Maud's eyes lit up. "I would be so grateful. I hope your veterinarian friend can prescribe something to help Mouse, because I'm very worried about him."

"I'm sure Midge will take good care of your dog. She always does. I can call her for you if you'd like."

"Thank you. That's very kind." Maud paused, as if deciding something, then said suddenly, "I'm sorry Herbert caused such a ruckus yesterday. He had no right to badger you the way he did."

"You know Mr. Grissom?" Faith asked, surprised.

"Oh yes," Maud answered with a resigned sigh. "I met him at a children's book conference. It was before he got so full of himself." She scrunched up her nose, as though something smelled bad.

"Have you seen Mr. or Mrs. Grissom today?" Faith asked.

"No. Not since yesterday afternoon."

Faith wondered where the couple could be.

"Please excuse me. I should go check on Mouse." Maud turned and walked away.

"Good luck with your dog," Faith called after her. She watched her retreating figure for a long moment after she was no longer visible.

So, Maud and Herbert knew each other. And clearly, Faith's new friend was not impressed.

"I have some calls to make nearby anyway," Midge explained. "It's no trouble to stop by the manor."

Faith had called Midge about Maud's dog and asked her over to the cottage for lunch. Now they sat in Faith's kitchen, enjoying paninis and jasmine tea.

"Thank you," Faith said. "Maud will be relieved. She's really worried."

"I'm partial to Chihuahuas like my sweet Atticus. And besides, you offered me lunch, so how could I refuse?" Midge, who hailed from Frog Eye, Alabama, sometimes slipped into phrases that accentuated her distinctive Southern accent. She sipped her tea like a true Southern belle, with her polished pinkie finger extended. Today she sported cranberry-colored nails with delicate white snowflakes on them.

"Her dog has the sniffles," Faith said. "And he weighs all of two pounds."

"Atticus weighs a little more, and he still can't see past his nose without his Doggles."

Doggles were very expensive dog glasses that Midge had bought to help her beloved pet with his waning eyesight.

"Has he given up trying to eat them yet?" Faith asked, laughing.

"They're growing on him," Midge said with a toss of her blonde hair. "So, what's the dog's name?"

"Mouse. The name is interesting since his owner has written an intriguing book about a mouse in the Bastille, of all places. I think it has great potential. She illustrated the story herself, and the drawings are delightful."

"Things are never dull at the manor, are they?" Midge remarked.

The events of the past few days flashed through Faith's mind. "No," she said and sighed deeply.

"That doesn't sound good." Midge pushed aside her sandwich plate and leaned back in her chair.

Faith shook her head. "Oh, it's just this rather difficult guest." Briefly she explained what had happened and that no one had seen Herbert yet that day. According to Marlene, he hadn't attended any morning workshops or lectures.

"Where do you think he is?" Midge asked.

"I don't know, but if he doesn't show, I doubt anyone will be sorry. And that parrot of his is the noisiest, most irksome—"

"Parrot?" Midge laughed. "How did Watson do with this irksome parrot?"

"Not very well, I'm afraid. He had a very bad day. Usually he gets along with other animals."

"Bribe him with some of these tunaroons." She reached into her black medical bag, imprinted with her initials in bright purple letters, and removed a small sack. "They should perk him up."

"Thanks," Faith said, accepting the treats. "Well, come on. I'll go with you to Maud's suite. She's expecting you. And who knows? We may run into Black Bart."

When Faith and Midge arrived at the Emily Dickinson Suite, Maud was waiting, carrying a somewhat lethargic mouse of a dog with big, weeping eyes.

At the sight of guests, the animal appeared startled and began to shake.

Of course, many small dogs—Chihuahuas in particular—always shivered, whether from actual cold or nervousness.

Midge took Mouse in her capable hands and began her examination, murmuring words of comfort to him. He calmed under her touch.

"I guess I didn't even know dogs could catch cold," Maud said as she petted the tiny dog's head.

"There are differences in the types of viruses that infect humans versus dogs," Midge said, "but the symptoms are basically the same—sneezing, runny nose, and watery eyes, like in Mouse's case. The illness is not communicable between species, so there's no need to worry about catching your dog's cold or vice versa."

Maud nodded.

Midge reached for her black bag. "I'm going to give you some electrolyte solution to mix with Mouse's water, which will help prevent dehydration. And this vitamin B complex should increase his appetite and boost his immune system." She removed the packages from her bag and handed them to Maud.

"Thank you," Maud said, nearly tearful.

"Let me know if Mouse gets any worse, but I think he'll be feeling better soon." Midge smiled warmly. "Enjoy the rest of the retreat."

When they had left the Dickinson suite, Faith hooked her arm through her friend's. "Mouse is a sweet little thing, isn't he?"

"He sure is."

"And you made his mama feel much better."

"I was glad to help," Midge said. "Feeling helpless over a pet is one of the worst feelings in the world."

"It really is. By the way, do you mind if we take a detour?" Faith asked.

Midge raised an eyebrow.

"I thought I'd stop by the Robert Louis Stevenson Suite," Faith explained. "That's where the Grissoms are staying."

The Robert Louis Stevenson Suite, with its treasure map border on brown-and-red walls, seemed appropriate for the would-be pirate. Some of the furniture was designed as treasure chests. Ships with tall masts sailed on high shelves.

"Perhaps they're resting or not feeling well," Faith continued. "I'll just check on them before I return to the library."

"I'll tag along," Midge said. "I can spare a few more minutes."

When they arrived at the suite, Faith tapped tentatively on the door, feeling like something of a voyeur. Guests should be given their privacy, and they had a right to choose which events they wanted to attend.

"They don't seem to be in," Midge said.

Faith knocked again, more firmly this time.

"Awk! Leaf over! Pity! More's the pity!"

"Harley's in there. At least he's not annoying the other guests with his ridiculous phrases." *Phrases that make no sense at all*, Faith thought. But she had no doubt the parrot had learned them by rote from his master.

They stood for several more seconds, listening to the bird squawking and rustling about, but no one answered the door.

Faith shrugged. "At least they haven't gone away for long—not without Harley."

"Is there something you wanted?"

Faith jumped at the voice, not having heard anyone approach.

Katrina Grissom, dressed in a long dark coat and a shawl, stared at them suspiciously.

"There you are. We were passing by," Faith said, then introduced Midge. "We hadn't seen you all day, and we were a bit worried."

Katrina shifted a package from one arm to the other. "I have been out shopping," she said shortly, shaking her braided hair free of the shawl. A fine mist of melting snowflakes glistened on her straw-colored hair. Her German accent grew more noticeable as she spoke. "Am I not free to go out shopping in the town?"

"Of course you are," Faith answered. "But the assistant manager of Castleton was concerned. Your husband hasn't attended any of the meals or sessions today."

Katrina shrugged. "I wouldn't know. I only came to this retreat because my husband told me to. I am not so much interested in books."

Faith glanced behind Katrina. "Is your husband with you?"

"I am alone. I went shopping with a friend who is also a guest here. I have not seen Herbie since yesterday afternoon." She pressed past Faith and Midge and put her key into the lock of the suite. "You must excuse me. I am very tired."

Harley screamed as Katrina opened the door.

"You mean he didn't come back to your suite last night?" Faith asked, stepping closer to prevent the door's quick close.

"My husband has his own ways. It is the way of the artist. *Entschuldigung, bitte,*" Katrina said, excusing herself with a dark look and closing the door.

"So much for hospitality," Midge said, pursing her fuchsia lips.

"So much for wedded bliss," Faith added.

So where is the troublesome artist? And if he didn't come back to his suite last night, what has he been up to?

6

The cat sniffed along the edge of the walkway behind the manor.

He had snuck out of the cottage while his human was having lunch with the owner of the delectable bakery, which was his all-time favorite. Even if the owner did occasionally put him on that slippery table and poke at his belly and peek into his ears, he forgave her. His human liked her. Besides, she supplied him with tunaroons, and it had been entirely too long since his last one. So, he'd gone exploring on his own. After all, a cat needs a snack.

Behind the manor was the best place to find tasty morsels. Every now and then, the humans who worked in the kitchen would drop something on their way to the big garbage container.

But it was tough going with all this snow. Not to mention, it was cold on his sensitive feet. He took a few steps and shook his paws. Then he took a few more steps and shook his paws again. He'd have quite a cleaning job to do when he got back to the cottage.

As he trudged along, he heard something. He snuck back behind a low wall, which in summer was often covered with fragrant green plants. He flicked his ears forward, listening.

Someone was coming.

He wrinkled his nose. It smelled like that human. The cat didn't like him. He was the one in the car with the big bird that fluttered and squawked.

He squinted. No bird and no hairy-faced human. It was just the human with the yellow hair and a big shawl.

And someone else, someone he didn't recognize. But the place was often littered with strange humans coming and going. He didn't usually mind. Most of the humans who came for a while and then went away *were quite respectful. Sometimes they brought pets—others of his kind to make things interesting.*

The yellow-haired human jumped back when the other one stepped out from behind a bush.

There was nothing respectful about the tone of their voices, which grew louder and louder. Had they no propriety?

If they spotted him, they might grab a broom and chase him away. The cat hunkered down until the yellow-haired human ran off.

The other one in the hat stood there glowering and eventually walked away in the opposite direction.

The cat craned his neck to peer around the wall.

Another human exited the back door of the manor, clutching something tightly.

He sniffed. It was nothing that smelled good.

The human glanced around, then stooped and shoved the box under the trash receptacle until the cat couldn't see it anymore.

So much for a tasty snack.

After thanking Midge for checking on Mouse and bidding her friend goodbye, Faith hurried downstairs to the library.

While she walked, she considered the awkward and disturbing confrontation with Katrina. To all appearances, Katrina and Herbert had differing interests and pursuits, but it was odd that she had no idea where her husband was, nor did she seem in the least concerned, even after she learned that he hadn't attended any meals or sessions at the retreat.

Faith recalled Katrina's expression the day her husband had ordered her back into the car with the frantic Harley. There was no fondness in the look. Sadly, she decided there was little harmony between the couple.

As Faith opened the library door, she wondered if anyone had checked to see if Herbert's car was in the parking lot. She would mention it to Marlene.

She had barely situated herself at her desk when the door opened. Faith glanced up to see Marlene and a tall, silver-haired man enter the room and stride toward her.

The man wore a fine pin-striped suit with a silk cravat tucked into the neck of a blue-green shirt. His face was unlined and youthful, at odds with the silver hair. He appeared to be in excellent shape, and Faith guessed he couldn't be more than forty-five.

The man stared at Faith, his lips forming a curious, wordless question. His eyes were very dark—the pupils blending with the irises so they glowed like obsidian gems.

Faith dropped the folder she had been perusing and got to her feet.

Marlene gave the man a wide, admiring smile. Her eyes glowed in the pink flush of her face. "I'd like you to meet Castleton's librarian, Faith Newberry." She stumbled slightly over Faith's last name in a rare show of flustered embarrassment. "Faith, this is Mr. Léon Delacroix, whom we have been expecting."

Clearly, Mr. Léon Delacroix had made quite an impression on the normally hypercontrolled assistant manager. Marlene seemed nothing short of giddy.

The man made a slight bow and lifted Faith's hand to his lips.

Faith nearly laughed in surprise at the old-world manners and the formality. Had she slipped into another century? Or was Léon being deliberately over the top? Who wore a cravat these days? But she had to admit it looked dashing.

"It's Leo. Just Leo," he said with a warm smile. "And I am honored to make your acquaintance."

"A pleasure, I'm sure," Faith said, settling her features into polite interest. At least he wasn't going to stand on ceremony, and he could, if he chose, employ regular speech. Kissing the hand, however, seemed completely and devastatingly French.

"Mr. Delacroix has only just arrived—well, a short time ago anyway," Marlene said, her voice a little higher than usual. "I'm sure he is very tired after his trip and would like to settle into his room before his lecture this evening on the place of fiction in literature. He will be occupying the Mark Twain Suite."

The luxurious Mark Twain Suite had recently been renovated. In honor of the remarkable Twain, the most modern accoutrements and design had been employed.

"I've told him how eager our writers and artists are to meet him." Again, Marlene gazed into his face with almost worshipful awe. "He doesn't want to keep them waiting any longer. I told him you were responsible for coordinating the exhibits, and he asked if you might be available to show them to him now."

Leo nodded ever so slightly, his dark eyes still sparkling with humor. He tucked his hands into the pockets of his suit. "If you can spare the time, Miss Newberry."

"Of course," she said. "Most of the guests are in a manuscript-sharing session. You can check out the exhibit without everyone hanging about and watching your reactions."

"Excellent," he said. He turned to Marlene. "Thank you for your attentiveness, Miss . . . ?"

Faith winced at the ignominy of his words. Not only was he dismissing Marlene, but he'd forgotten her name.

The assistant manager drew her eyebrows together with unconcealed displeasure, but she quickly rallied. "Marlene. Just Marlene," she managed, mimicking the style of his earlier introduction. She extracted a business card from her pocket and handed it to him with trembling fingers.

Faith had never seen Marlene so flustered. She was clearly smitten with Mr. Léon Delacroix.

"Miss Newberry will take good care of you, but please don't hesitate to call on me anytime." Marlene turned and strode away.

Faith couldn't help herself from joining in the name game.

"It's Faith. Just Faith." Glancing at Leo, she detected amusement in his eyes.

At that moment, Watson appeared out of nowhere and leaped onto Faith's desk. He plunked down unceremoniously and peered at Leo as though to determine what sort of human he might be.

The cat occasionally leaped onto her desk. Once or twice he had lofted himself onto Marlene's desk at no small threat to his furry person.

"What are you doing up there?" she scolded Watson with more surprise than severity. "Get down."

"Your cat?" Leo asked.

Faith nodded. "Watson. I'd say he's usually better behaved, but he is a cat, and cats do as they wish."

"He's a very handsome specimen," he observed, stooping to hold out his hand.

Watson pranced away from Leo without a backward glance.

"I'm sorry. That wasn't very friendly of him."

"Cats usually have minds of their own," Leo said. "I think it's very accommodating of Mr. Jaxon to allow guests to bring their pets. Guests *and* staff," he amended, stroking his chin thoughtfully. "Watson, eh? As in Sherlock Holmes's sidekick?"

"Yes. He's an extremely clever cat. He fended for himself after he was abandoned as a kitten. When I found him, the name seemed to fit." Faith straightened some papers on her desk, which had been mussed by Watson's presence. "Well, shall we have a look at the exhibits?"

"After you," he said, extending a long, well-groomed hand.

It was a relief to move, to be out from under the scrutiny of this handsome, polished man. She walked a little ahead of him, aware of him off to her right shoulder, and led him to the exhibit hall.

"Well done," Leo said as he studied the tables with their colorful contents. From the inside pocket of his suit, he withdrew a shiny smartphone and began tapping, obviously taking notes.

Faith stood aside as he swept along the double row of tables rather swiftly, perhaps getting an overview to inspect them much more closely later. He seemed more interested in scanning the area, as though searching for something in particular.

"Are all the exhibits set up?" he asked.

"I believe so," Faith said a bit tentatively, for Herbert could still be awaiting his portfolio. But even if that was the case, there was plenty of time. The exhibits would remain for the duration of the retreat.

Leo tipped his head slightly and raised one dark eyebrow yet untouched with silver. He might have perceived her hesitance but made no comment. Instead, he nodded at some illustrations of horses at Kip's table. "These are interesting. I look forward to studying this exhibit and the others more closely in the coming days."

"I'm glad to hear it," Faith said.

"I wonder if there might be a cup of coffee available," he remarked. "And might you kindly have a few minutes to share one with me?"

"Certainly," Faith said, trying not to show her surprise. Surely Marlene had offered refreshments to her special guest upon his arrival. She ushered Leo into the salon.

Compared to most of the massive rooms in the manor, the salon felt cozy with its wood floors and pale walls. Guests would be breaking for refreshments any moment now and begin gathering at the festive round tables that had been set up. Fresh pastries, created by Brooke and her helpers, were already being carted in.

"Have you worked at Castleton Manor long?" Leo asked when they were seated with cups of steaming coffee.

Faith leaned back in her chair, wondering why his presence should unnerve her. "Long enough to know I am extremely fortunate. The Jaxon family's dedication to literature and to making this place available to guests from all over is remarkable. It's their family mansion, but they love having people around—people and pets, as you have already noted." She wrapped her hands around the cup, grateful for its solid warmth. "I'm very happy here."

He smiled. "And from what I've heard, they are fortunate to have you."

She felt a slight warming of her cheeks at his closer glance. "Mr. Jaxon was pleased when he learned that you were willing to participate in this retreat. It means a great deal to writers and artists to have the attention of a notable publisher."

"We're starting a subsidiary of our Canadian company here in the United States," Leo said. "We're quite small yet, but we're looking for new talent. Since we'll be located in New York, I was pleased to offer my services when I heard of this conference."

Faith realized she knew little about Maple Publishing of Quebec—or about Léon Delacroix. She had thought only of their good fortune to have a representative of a distinguished Canadian publisher attend this retreat for children's writers and artists.

If she hadn't been so wrapped up in helping Eileen organize the children's afternoon on top of her other duties, she might have looked up the company in order to be able to make intelligent conversation with him about his work.

She made a mental note to research him and his company at the earliest opportunity as guests began filing into the salon. They chatted amiably as they helped themselves to the refreshments and took seats at the tables.

Among them was Wolfe, appearing strong and self-assured in an open-collar white shirt and gray trousers. He approached their table, then extended a hand to Leo. "Wolfe Jaxon. It's a pleasure to have you here at Castleton, Mr. Delacroix."

Leo shook Wolfe's hand. "Thank you. I'm glad to be here."

Wolfe glanced from Leo to Faith. "I see you've met our librarian," he said.

"Indeed," Leo responded. "I'm afraid I have taken advantage of her time and hospitality. She gave me my first look at the wonderful exhibits prepared by your guests. I can see that you have some fine artists present."

The guests were mingling, enjoying the refreshments, and frequently turning their way and whispering, no doubt about the handsome publishing representative with silver hair and old-world cravat who had finally arrived.

Wolfe seemed momentarily caught up in thought. Then he said abruptly, "Great. Glad to hear it. Is everything to your liking so far?"

Leo nodded.

"Would you like the five-dollar tour of the place?" Wolfe asked. "I'd be glad to show you around."

"*Oui.* I would indeed," Leo responded with the first hint of French.

"*Viens avec moi*," Wolfe said.

Faith recalled the phrase from her high school French class. It meant "Come with me."

Both men thanked her and left the salon.

As she stared after them, she felt bewildered and amused along with a host of other emotions.

She suddenly became aware of a hand on her shoulder.

Brooke swept into the chair across from her. "That must be the famous Léon Delacroix we've been hearing about." Her face glowed, eyes glittering. "How do you say 'hubba-hubba' in French?"

Faith laughed, glad for a sound reason to release her churning emotions. "I think that one's pretty universal." When was the last time she'd heard that archaic phrase? But it was so like Brooke, the quintessential romantic.

"Is he married?"

Faith shrugged. She'd seen no ring on those immaculate fingers, but who could know?

Brooke liked to entertain her friends with accounts of her latest date, but Faith knew Brooke was intentional about relationships and took these things seriously, though she frequently made light of them. Faith had a wild thought: *What would Diva and Bling make of Léon Delacroix?*

"It's clear that he's got an eye for you," Brooke teased. "Wolfe had better watch out."

"Don't start that again," Faith warned, then deliberately derailed the subject of male attractions. "You look tired. Is everything all right?"

"Oh, I'm fine," Brooke said. "I didn't sleep too well last night, and I've been working late to get ready for the Christmas party."

"You work too hard," Faith said. "Has Angelina been pulling her weight?" The last time they'd talked, Brooke had mentioned the part-time helper hadn't shown up to work yet.

"She's a very hard worker," Brooke said. Then she heaved a sigh. "But I wish she were a bit more open. All she wants to do is stay in the kitchen. I can hardly get her to go out for a break or even to take things outside to the trash."

"Really? That's strange."

Brooke sighed again. "I asked her to set out the pastries a little while ago, and she virtually said no. I know she isn't lazy. She's just so awkward around people. She doesn't let Kevin go out by himself either if she can help it. She's even been taking him to school herself lately."

"Maybe she's not the right sort of help," Faith said tentatively.

Brooke's eyes clouded. "She seemed perfect at first. I know she has concerns at home—young Kevin and of course, money." She shrugged. "She slips in and back out like a thief in the night, but in between she works like a demon in the kitchen."

Faith pondered this and worried about her friend.

Brooke got up. "And that's what I've got to do," she said, her quandary over Angelina apparently pushed aside for the moment. She shook her finger at Faith. "Keep your guard up. Those two may come to blows over you." And she rushed off before Faith could object to her romantic nonsense.

Faith considered Angelina's bizarre actions. What was going on with the woman? Why did she refuse to take pastries into the salon, where perfectly normal and even pleasant people were gathered?

Brooke had remarked that Angelina slipped in and out like a thief in the night. Why? Had there been other episodes of near fainting? Was the single mother ill?

Midge was right. Things were never dull at the manor.

7

Brooke outdid herself at dinner that night. Creamy asparagus soup was followed by expertly made lobster risotto. The main course—pan-seared filet mignon with garlic and herb butter, accompanied by roasted root vegetables and baby potatoes—melted in Faith's mouth.

She was sure she couldn't manage another bite, but then a rich pavlova topped with fresh berries was served, and she found herself suddenly able to polish it off with no trouble, especially after she discovered the tart lemon curd inside.

After dinner, Faith stayed at the manor to listen to Leo Delacroix's lecture on the place of fiction in literature.

Marlene, still appearing a bit rattled, gave a few announcements, then briefly summarized the speaker's impressive bio.

Leo had earned a master's degree in English literature from a prestigious university in Ottawa. He had edited several publications, including a line of academic books for children, and currently he was the acquisitions director of children's books for the family-owned Maple Publishing in Quebec.

The audience applauded, giving Leo a warm welcome.

Marlene gave Leo an admiring look when he approached the podium, then took her seat.

"Thank you, Ms. Russell," Leo said, then launched directly into his lecture. "What is the point of literary fiction? Shouldn't one rather read a biography or a book on how to wire lamps? Shouldn't we spend our time absorbing something that is true?"

He scanned the audience. "Is *Sense and Sensibility* not true? Did Joseph Conrad, exploring the *Heart of Darkness* through fiction, not delve deeply into truth? Did not Charles Dickens graphically incorporate terrible and wondrous truth in *Oliver Twist* and *A Tale of Two Cities*?"

Leo's silver hair gleamed in the overhead light, and when he lowered his head for effect, his sculpted lips inexorably drew the eye. "Or what of Herman Melville writing about the great conflict between man and beast? He unearthed a deeper truth in *Moby-Dick* than we are able to find in any number of how-to books. Ladies and gentlemen, I would argue that fiction is another way to explore truth."

Leo kept his audience riveted. Faith found herself listening less to the content of the lecture than to its elocution. He occasionally allowed his French accent to come to the fore.

Though the subject was elementary, Leo presented a compelling thesis. "Great meaning rarely issues from science alone," he stated. "As Hamlet declared, 'There are more things in heaven and earth, Horatio, than are dreamt of in your philosophy.'"

Several times during the talk Leo glanced in Faith's direction, his gaze more intrusive than was comfortable. Or was she imagining it? She shook her head to dismiss the ridiculous notion. She was only flattering herself.

When Leo was finished, he received a standing ovation.

Then hot apple cider and gingerbread cake were served. Faith noticed that several members of Leo's admiring audience, including Patsy, angled to sit closer to him.

Faith was tired and longed for the solace of her cottage, so she skipped the refreshments and returned to the library. She cleared her desk, gathered Watson from his forays among the library's nooks and crannies, and walked out into the white wonderland of the manor's grounds.

The sky was a cloud-heavy ebony that allowed for the barest hint of moon and no starlight. An unnamed tension hung in the chilly air, as though the earth were holding its breath.

She reveled in the crunch of snow under her feet, the invigorating cold that at first felt so welcome on her face after hours spent indoors. Soon it would sting and redden unprotected skin. At least the snow had finally stopped, but it had left a thick legacy for the property staff to clear.

As Faith relished the walk home through the snow-covered grounds with her cat, her thoughts turned to the Grissoms.

Herbert had not made an appearance all day, and his absence was becoming harder to ignore.

During a midafternoon break, Marlene had grilled Katrina in her efficient, determined manner.

Katrina had claimed she had phoned home and checked with friends, but she had learned nothing about her husband's whereabouts. Then she had insisted that it wasn't unusual for Herbie to go off by himself, especially when he was upset, as he had been the previous day.

Faith had almost expected Herbert to storm into the banquet hall during dinner or to skulk in, grousing under his breath about everyone and everything at the manor that didn't quite suit him. But now, late into the evening, there was still no sign of him.

While Faith had enjoyed the relative peace of hours without the obnoxious artist causing an uproar, the prospect that something bad had happened to him filled her with dread. She wondered whether anyone had grown concerned enough to inform the police.

Watson had been tripping along behind her, occasionally venturing off the path to poke his nose into something that interested him.

The cat had grown used to Cape Cod winters and even seemed to enjoy the aftermath of a storm. He might be part dog the way he pushed snow up with his nose, then shook it off his whiskers. He was all cat, however, when it came to cold, wet paws. Still, curiosity generally overruled his fussier side.

She turned to check his location, but despite his black coat, he was invisible against the white backdrop.

What was so much fun as a romp in the snow? The cat loved to push the snow up with his nose—something humans thought only dogs did. What did they know? A clever feline could simply shake his whiskers, lick away any resisting substance, and be ready to go again.

After all, one could find the most intriguing objects hidden beneath the white stuff. And if he was thirsty, snow filled the bill.

"Rumpy!" his person called.

He supposed he should go back, but humans missed so many treasures simply walking with their noses in the air and never bothering to see what lay underfoot.

He galloped toward one of the fountains. He loved to pretend he was a daring explorer testing his courage before taking the polar plunge. Which he never actually did, of course. It was much too cold, and really, he didn't like getting wet. It was just that things were so tempting, especially when they were hidden.

There was no water spraying up now—not even any water to dance around. It was only a big, wide bowl with snow in the bottom.

Then he smelled something he did not like. He stopped, shook his paws against the cold, and twitched his whiskers.

What was that?

Something down there had invaded his territory.

"Rumpy," Faith called again. *I might as well talk to the wind.* Then, thanks to the outdoor lighting on the grounds, she spotted Watson walking along the wide base of the Peter Pan fountain.

The whimsical fountain was dedicated to perpetual life—to never growing old, to accepting the joys of existence with open arms and a trusting heart. In the summer, its crystal waters erupted and sprayed back into a wide, shallow pool.

Around the base and atop the center pole of the fountain were cherubic figures now coated with snow. All lay sleeping, drained of life-giving water, with a thick cedar hedge guarding their privacy.

"Come on, Watson!" Faith called, irritated that her cat had made such a detour. "Time to go home. Midge brought tunaroons," she added, hoping to entice him.

Then she raised her voice and called his name again, for the snow muffled her voice as though she spoke through a pillow.

But if the cat had heard, his selective obedience was in full play.

What was so interesting that he was willing to wade through the snow, forgoing the prospect of a warm fire in their cozy cottage?

Reluctantly, she made her way to the cedar hedge and stepped through the opening.

The cat stood staring down from his perch on the ledge of the fountain, not moving at all. His little stub of a tail seemed to droop. He glanced up at her and meowed.

Perhaps a chipmunk had scampered across the white basin and dared Watson for a chase. Or maybe a purple finch, foraging in the snow for an edible tidbit, had captured his attention.

"Watson, what are you—" She stopped, her breath caught in her throat.

There in the shallow pool something lay partially buried in the snow. Something as dark and thick as a tree limb stuck out from the white mound. And there was a boot at its end.

Faith stared, frozen to the spot, her arms and legs paralyzed for what seemed like an eternity. In the deep silence that wrapped around her, she heard an owl's mournful dirge echoing and falling away.

"Oh no!" The words ripped from her throat when she saw crystallized blood on the white ground. She almost dropped to her knees.

Even before she stumbled over to the basin, she knew exactly what she was seeing.

Herbert Grissom was dead.

8

Faith recoiled, almost falling backward. Then she spotted the odd, curved cutlass unsheathed from the holster at Herbert's hip and gleaming in the snow. Its blade was stained with blood.

The weapon had been no rubber toy, no plasticized costume as she had assumed. It was real, and it had killed him.

The strangest sensation came over her. She wanted to wipe the snow from Herbert's face and tell him it was time to wake up. Harley needed him.

But Herbert Grissom would never need his pet parrot or his wife or anyone ever again.

Through the pounding in her brain, she reached into the pocket of her coat and removed her phone. She punched in 911 with trembling fingers.

"There's a body in the snow at Castleton Manor." She heard her voice as though from somewhere outside herself.

The operator asked her several questions, and she answered them the best she could.

"The police and paramedics will be there in a few minutes," the operator promised. "Why don't you wait for them inside the manor?"

Faith disconnected the call and scooped up Watson in her arms. She stared down for a long moment, profoundly sad. The loss of life was always tragic, even if that life had not been particularly pleasant. Then, clutching the cat close to her chest, she hurried toward the manor.

She rushed through the topiaries, along the winding path, and then up toward the grand entrance surrounded by the elegant loggia where guests often took the evening air. No one would be watching there tonight. It was too cold.

Light bathed the graceful structure. The guests would be breaking up now and heading to their elegant rooms for a night's rest, wrapped in the delight of the day's adventures, the evening's pleasant occupation. They had been discussing the books they loved, the craft they pursued—all unaware of the tragedy that had occurred just a short distance away.

When she entered the Great Hall Gallery, Watson wiggled from her arms and scampered off toward the Agatha Christie statue.

Some of the guests were milling around and talking.

Wolfe turned from the group of guests he was speaking with and saw Faith standing there. He must have seen in her face that something was wrong, because he walked over to her, concern in his eyes, and led her away from the crowd of curious faces with a gentle hand on her elbow.

No one moved or spoke, but she was sure they knew something of import had occurred and they were not likely to go off to sleep anytime soon. And when sirens began to blare, they would converge to discover the reason.

Wolfe escorted Faith down the hall, and Marlene wordlessly followed them.

Inside the library, Wolfe ushered Faith to a chair. "What's wrong?"

Faith drew in her breath and swallowed the sob that tore at her throat. "It's Herbert Grissom. He's at the Peter Pan fountain. And he's dead."

Marlene gasped.

Then the distant drone of a siren sounded.

"You called 911?" Wolfe asked gently.

Faith nodded, not trusting herself to speak.

"Was anyone else with you?" Wolfe continued.

"Just Watson." Faith bit her lip. "He wandered off the path, and I followed him to the fountain. That's where I found Herbert."

"Did you see anyone else in the area?" Wolfe persisted.

Faith shook her head. "Herbert's alone out there."

"Not for long. The police are coming, and I'm going out to meet them." Wolfe turned to Marlene and said, "Stay with Faith."

"I'll go with you," Faith volunteered, and she started to rise from her seat.

"The chief will want to talk to you soon," he said firmly. "Just sit for a little while. You've had quite an evening already." He gestured to Marlene, clearly turning Faith over to her care. Then he left, closing the library door behind him.

Marlene sat down across from her on one of the plush armchairs. Faith knew the assistant manager worked with dogged care and determination to make certain no untoward episodes occurred. But the worst had happened despite her efforts. Soon the guests would hover near the library, and she would have to handle the situation.

"I can't believe it," Faith began. "It's a dreadful thing. A terrible waste." The sight of the artist lying there reeled through her mind. What had happened? Had he been so desperate over something in his life that he had . . . ? Or had someone else done this awful thing?

"Did you see anyone?" Marlene asked. Perhaps realizing that the question had already been posed and answered, she asked, "How long do you think he's been dead?"

"I have no idea," Faith said. "I hope the coroner will be able to tell us, though when a body has been buried in ice and snow, it complicates things. The coroner won't be able to use body temperature to determine it. Plus, decomposition is slower, and it's harder to tell." Faith swallowed, trying to imagine Herbert Grissom silent—that flamboyant voice stopped, the animated body still clothed in pirate attire. A question popped into her mind: What would Katrina think?

"We need to tell his wife immediately," Marlene said, as though their thoughts had coincided. She frowned, then chewed thoughtfully on her lower lip. "Do you think she did it?"

Faith remembered what she had seen only a few hours earlier—the hostility in Katrina's cold blue eyes that had chilled her. But why would Katrina do it? And why in such a public place? Had something happened to make her snap? Faith halted her own thoughts. It was foolish to speculate at this point.

"She didn't seem concerned that he was missing," Marlene said somewhat scornfully.

"We don't know that anyone killed him," Faith said. She realized the shock had lifted, and her natural capacity for mystery was showing itself. "But if it was murder, Katrina would most likely be one of the chief suspects." She sighed. "Along with me." After all, she had discovered the body.

Chief Andy Garris wouldn't really suspect Faith, of course. What reason would she have to harm Herbert? She would hardly commit murder over a tiny scratch on her car's bumper.

But everyone would be questioned and all motives considered. Katrina was Herbert's wife, and from what Faith had seen, she wouldn't exactly call their marriage a fairy tale.

There was also Herbert's former partner, author Felix Anderson. The enmity between the pair had been plain to see, though she had been the only one to witness their heated argument.

Another thought occurred to her. Kip Rudyard had clearly disliked Herbert. She recalled the commotion over the missing portfolio and how Kip and Herbert had mocked each other unmercifully. How well were the two illustrators acquainted?

How well did any of the guests know Herbert?

Even sweet grandmotherly Maud had a history with the difficult artist. Surely, there was no way the elderly woman could overpower a strong man like Herbert, even if she wanted to. Yet stranger things had occurred.

Faith drew a deep breath. Discovering what had happened to Herbert would hang over the retreat's atmosphere like an oppressive cloud.

And it couldn't have occurred at a worse time. On Saturday, the children would arrive at the manor for an afternoon of Christmas merriment—sleigh rides, story reading, a gala party—amid an ongoing police investigation. Faith pictured yellow tape around the Peter Pan fountain and police officers invading the splendid grounds.

Somehow they must keep the ugly tentacles of this tragedy from spoiling the children's day.

9

An hour had passed since Faith had burst into the manor with the terrible news of Herbert's demise. The police and the paramedics, who had responded quickly, had gone directly to the site.

Now Chief Andy Garris entered the library. In his late fifties, he was remarkably toned, as one might expect from a former marine, and he had a forceful bearing. But Faith also knew the chief to be a kind and intelligent man, and she respected him.

The chief walked over to where Faith and Marlene were sitting. "Wolfe will be escorting the guests in here so I can tell them what happened."

Marlene nodded.

Then the door opened again, and Wolfe ushered the guests inside. They gathered in the main area as Wolfe directed.

Faith saw no sign of Katrina, but it was likely that she had been kept apart from the others and the news brought first to her as next of kin.

Officer Jan Rooney would likely be the one chosen to talk to Herbert's wife. She was an empathetic and skilled member of Lighthouse Bay's police department. Faith was sure the officer would miss nothing while giving off a comforting air.

The guests grew suddenly silent.

The grandfather clock struck eleven, the sound echoing dolefully through the room.

Chief Garris caught Faith's eye as he walked to the front of the assembled group.

She tried to read the expression in the chief's sharp blue eyes, but it was guarded, serious.

"It's my sad duty," Garris began, "to tell you that one of your fellow guests has been found dead. We understand the victim, Mr. Herbert Grissom, has been missing since yesterday. The cause of death appears to be a wound from a short sword, which was part of the costume the artist was wearing at the time. We are treating his death as a possible homicide."

A collective gasp went up from the guests.

Maud put a trembling hand to her mouth. With the other hand, she snuggled Mouse. The tiny Chihuahua was obviously better after Midge's ministrations. His enormous bulging eyes were bright, but he still shivered.

Patsy wrapped her arms around her chest and leaned forward, red hair forming curtains for her angular face. Just that morning her face had been alive with pleasure as she read the 1912 edition of "'Twas the Night Before Christmas." Now her freckles stood out as she paled. She absentmindedly petted the Pekingese curled up in her lap.

Leo leaned against a shelf of books at the rear of the library. He had removed his pin-striped suit jacket and loosened the cravat at his neck. Faith read nothing in the coal-like eyes, but she thought he appeared tired. No doubt traveling to the manor and giving a lecture that same evening had worn him down. The guests had also clamored for his attention—some, like Patsy, more ardently than others.

Faith turned back to Chief Garris.

"Mrs. Grissom has been informed." The chief glanced around the room before continuing, his expression stern. "Our department has begun an investigation, which may take some time. We will expect full cooperation from all of you, as has been promised by Mr. Jaxon. We will be taking a statement from each of you tomorrow. It is requested that none of you leave Lighthouse Bay until further notice."

"What are you saying? We're going to be holed up here in this burg?" Kip stood, his face flushed, thick eyebrows drawn together. He'd rolled up the sleeves of his shirt, revealing the markings of his dragon tattoo. "Grisly Grissom is at it again," he muttered under his breath.

Kip was a most unlikely member of this retreat—tough-talking, crass, and almost slovenly in dress, though he was obviously financially able to afford a luxury resort. Faith recalled their earlier discussion and the man's apparent antipathy to colleagues who had become successful, which he seemed to assume had happened through some means other than their talent.

"Mr. Rudyard," Wolfe said sternly, "you must understand that when something of this nature happens, there has to be an investigation. Everyone needs to help by offering what information they might have." He gave the man a penetrating look. "You're here for the retreat anyway. You've paid for the whole week. We hope things will progress quickly, but we will need full cooperation to make that happen."

Kip sat down again and thrust his fingers through his red hair in an aggrieved gesture. He grumbled to an elderly gentleman next to him and then mercifully went silent.

"This is something no one could have predicted," Wolfe said. "I am deeply sorry this has happened. I want you all to know that we will do everything we can to assist you and to carry on with the retreat as scheduled. Every courtesy will be extended to Mrs. Grissom, and we trust you will afford her the privacy she will need while dealing with her loss."

At a nod from Chief Garris, Marlene and Wolfe ushered the solemn guests from the library.

Moments later, only Chief Garris remained. He came toward Faith, both hands tucked into his trouser pockets, his jacket unzipped. He hadn't removed it upon entering the library with Wolfe. No doubt he was soaking up needed heat after being outside.

For her part, Faith felt a cold no amount of heat was likely to affect.

The chief stopped and stood at her side. He said nothing for several seconds. Then he turned to face her. "Are you all right?"

She nodded. It felt good to have him here. As usual, he was a solid bulwark in the storm.

There had been other crimes to solve at Castleton Manor, and indeed she had found herself involved. She had even been considered a chief suspect in a crime when she first arrived in Lighthouse Bay.

Touching her elbow, Garris said kindly, "My car's right outside. I'll take you home. We can talk on the way."

Watson, who had quickly returned to Faith's side, dutifully followed.

Faith picked him up and carried him outside.

"I understand Mr. Grissom has ruffled a few feathers since he's been here," the chief said when they piled into his cruiser.

"Even before he got here," Faith affirmed.

"What do you mean?" Garris asked as he headed toward Faith's cottage.

"We met outside Snickerdoodles," Faith answered. "I was waiting for Eileen in my car when Herbert pulled in behind me—only he didn't stop soon enough and rear-ended me."

"Then what happened?"

Faith sketched in the details, including the animal highlights. "Herbert blamed me—well, Watson actually. He said my cat had gotten Harley—that's his pet parrot—so upset it distracted him."

"He sounds like quite a character," Chief Garris remarked. "We have learned that he was in the area two days prior to checking in at Castleton. He and his wife stayed at a hotel up the coast, a few miles from Lighthouse Bay. Do you have any idea why?"

Faith shook her head.

"Tell me about the pirate getup he was in. Was there a costume party at the manor?"

"No, it's part of his artist's persona, I guess," Faith said. "He was going to participate in an exhibit where artists and writers showcase their work. Herbert did a lot of action illustrations. He's known for his drawings of pirates from a series of children's stories. He was wearing that outfit the last time we saw him."

"Wolfe said he had no idea the sword was real," the chief mused. "He wouldn't have allowed it on the grounds if he had known."

"Do you think it's possible that Herbert might have stabbed himself?" Faith asked. "Maybe by accident?"

"We don't think so," he said, rubbing his jaw with a big hand. "Someone bent on suicide would likely find an easier way. Besides, from what I hear, Mr. Grissom doesn't seem the type. And it appears unlikely it was an accident, but the jury's still out on that."

They arrived at the cottage and sat silently in the car for a moment.

Then the chief added, "It's not easy to figure what might have happened. An awful lot of snow fell, covering up footprints and any objects that might have been left behind. And we don't know exactly how long Mr. Grissom was out there." He paused. "We found your footprints, of course—and Watson's."

"I know I probably messed up the scene," Faith admitted. "I brushed snow away to see what was underneath. Even though I knew he was gone when I saw part of his leg sticking out, I couldn't leave without being sure there was nothing I could do." She felt a lump swelling in her throat. "I'm sorry."

"You couldn't have known it was a crime scene, and you did what anyone would do when you saw someone who might need help," Garris assured her. "Go inside and get some rest. Tomorrow morning I'd like you to come to the station and answer a few more questions."

"Of course," she said.

There was a great deal more Faith should tell him, like the absence of Katrina for most of the day and her apparent unconcern for her husband. And the police probably didn't know about Felix Anderson and his argument with Herbert before the welcome dinner.

Someone had killed Herbert Grissom, taken away any opportunity of realizing a dream or doing the good he might have done in the world. There should be justice for him. She had a duty to do her part.

She sighed, suddenly deeply tired.

"I'll see you tomorrow," the chief said. "Call and we can work out a time."

"Thanks. I know you'll find the truth—whatever it may mean."

"Oh, sweetheart, come in here!" Eileen ran to the door of the Candle House Library and pulled Faith into her arms.

Faith returned the warm hug. She was careful not to press too close, knowing her aunt's rheumatoid arthritis was often painful.

"Brooke called me this morning and told me what happened." Eileen stepped back and studied her niece. "Are you all right?"

"I'm fine," Faith said. "Even better for seeing my favorite aunt."

"It must have been awful for you. Who would have thought that grouchy man with his noisy bird would end up dead? I'm so sorry for him, despite the way he acted and how he treated you. He was not my idea of a gentleman. But I'm sorry for you too, having to find him like that."

"It was quite a night, I can tell you," Faith said, removing her coat. "And this morning has been a little stressful. I just talked to Chief Garris at the station, and he took my statement." She smiled. "He offered me coffee, but I wanted to wait for yours."

"Absolutely. I also have some chocolate walnut cookies from Snickerdoodles. Let's go back to my office." Eileen stopped at the desk and told Gail, one of the part-time employees, that she was taking a break.

Gail nodded and resumed helping a woman choose a new series for her granddaughter to read.

Faith gazed around the library. It was still early, and only a few seniors were browsing the shelves or reading.

The privately funded library was housed in a quaint three-story stone building. At one time, it had been used for small-scale candle manufacturing. Some of the windows featured original glass, and there were massive wood beams and a great stone fireplace surrounded by cozy reading chairs. Patrons loved to curl up with their books and a delicious treat from nearby Snickerdoodles.

Faith followed Eileen past the children's room decorated half like a castle and half like a pirate ship. *Herbert would probably feel at home in that room*, she thought sadly.

Eileen led Faith to her office, and Faith hung up her coat and took a seat at the round table in the corner.

Eileen brought her much-anticipated coffee and a plate of cookies over to the table and sat down.

"I know we've all been busy," Faith said, helping herself to a cookie. "But I'm so ready for a meeting of the book club."

"We'll have a lot to talk about. But you could fill me in on a few things right now. What do you think happened to Mr. Grissom?" Eileen wasn't the gossipy sort, but she was a lifelong resident of the area, and she liked to know what was going on.

Faith took a bite of her cookie, then described how she and Watson had been walking home after the evening lecture and found the artist mostly buried in snow at the Peter Pan fountain next to a cutlass. "The police are now treating it as a homicide."

Eileen stared at Faith. "Murder? It was a real cutlass?"

Faith nodded. "We all thought it was some prop that was part of his costume."

"That's unbelievable. And they're sure it's murder?"

"According to the chief, suicide has been ruled out, based on the angle of the wound in Herbert's chest."

"It's so terrible." Eileen shuddered. "Have they determined the time of death yet?"

"They think sometime between one and three on Wednesday morning."

"You didn't find him until that evening."

"Yes, it was a long time for him to lie beneath the snow and ice,"

Faith responded, shivering. "Besides that, snow erased any footprints that were made before mine."

"Do they have any leads?"

"I don't know. Today the police will be taking statements from all the guests and the staff."

"Do you have any suspicions about who the murderer could be?"

"I told the police about Felix Anderson. He and Herbert were partners—writer and artist—of the Perry and the Pirate series. Herbert essentially fired Felix. They had quite a disagreement that Watson and I inadvertently witnessed before the welcome dinner."

"What did they argue about?"

"Herbert berated Felix and said that people bought his books only because of the great illustrations in them," Faith answered. "He claimed Felix couldn't get anywhere as a writer without him."

"You think Felix murdered Herbert out of revenge?" Eileen asked, brown eyes wide. "What kind of man is he?"

"From what I've seen, Felix seems pretty ordinary. He's not what you'd expect after reading one of his books. He seems rather reserved, and he's very thin."

"Looks can be deceiving," Eileen reminded her. "Do you think Felix knew Herbert would be at the retreat?"

"I don't think so. Felix accused Herbert of attending because of him," Faith said. "We definitely need to learn more about Felix."

Eileen's eyes took on a sharper gleam, and Faith knew her aunt was anxious to do some Internet research. She was sure Eileen's fingers would fly over the keyboard as soon as she had a spare moment.

Eileen nodded. "The man certainly bears watching. And of course, you have a front-row seat right there at the manor."

"Yes, I plan to do some sleuthing." Faith swallowed. "Then there's Herbert's wife, Katrina. She was with Herbert when he slammed into my car."

"I remember her. Where was she when everything happened?"

"During the time Herbert was missing—along with his portfolio, by the way—she said she went shopping," Faith replied. "Midge and I ran into her and asked if she'd heard from Herbert. She said she hadn't, and she didn't seem too happy about our snooping around her door."

"Does her alibi hold up?"

"It turns out that she did go shopping with one of the other wives who wasn't directly involved in the conference part of the retreat. Officer Rooney confirmed it, but there was plenty of time when she could have broken away and gone after Herbie, as she called him."

"I'd put my money on her," Eileen said. "The day I saw them, it didn't appear that she and her husband were exactly what you'd call close. And when Herbert told her to get back into the car, she glared daggers at him. Remember?"

"Clearly," Faith murmured. "Speaking of money, Katrina stands to gain a substantial sum now that her husband is dead. She'll receive his life insurance policy for $350,000 and whatever he left her in his will."

Eileen whistled through her teeth. "I'd say that puts her in the number one spot."

"But most couples have life insurance policies on each other," Faith reasoned.

"True. Do you know how long they've been married?"

"The chief says they've been married for only four years. Herbert and Katrina met in New York when she was fresh off the boat from Quedlinburg. It's in the Harz district of Germany and one of the most well-preserved medieval and renaissance towns in the world."

"Imagine that." Eileen sipped her coffee. "I wonder if Herbert had any other relatives, maybe even a former wife or two. The police will be all over it, I should imagine. Since he was a prominent illustrator, it should be easy to find more information about him."

"The police will be all over. Period. That's what's worrying me,"

Faith said. "We need to somehow make the day special for the children and keep them from the sordid mess of a police investigation, especially one about a murder."

"You're right. It has to be a perfect afternoon of holiday fun and—"

Someone knocked on the door of Eileen's office.

Eileen got up and opened the door. "Well, hello, Kevin," she said in surprise.

Faith recognized the ten-year-old boy she had met the day of her run-in with Herbert Grissom. Angelina's son. His dark curls lay over his forehead, all but obscuring one brown eye. His jacket flared open, and his shoelaces hung over his sneakers like cooked spaghetti. A grin spread across his sweet face, and she saw that he had a dimple in his chin—almost a cleft. It gave him an unusual but distinctive look.

"Hi, Mrs. Piper. I came to return this," he said, holding up a book about hockey.

"You could have returned it at the front desk."

"I know, but I wanted to say hi to you."

"I'm glad you did." Eileen smiled. "What did you think of the book?"

Kevin shrugged. "It was okay, but I liked the other one better."

"You remember my niece, don't you?" Eileen gestured to Faith.

"Sure. The lady with the cat who looks like he's wearing a fancy suit. Hello."

Faith grinned.

"How come you're not in school today, Kevin?" Eileen asked.

He shuffled his feet, then stuffed his hands into the pockets of his jacket. "My mom doesn't feel good. She needed me and said I should stay home."

"Is she all right?" Eileen asked casually. Faith read the concern in her aunt's eyes.

"Yeah. She's sleeping now, so I came to bring the book back." Kevin stared at the floor as though he'd done something he shouldn't.

So Angelina wasn't feeling well today. Brooke had been without her helper for the morning shift again.

What was really wrong with Kevin's mother?

And what would the hockey-loving boy do if something happened to her?

10

Faith was finishing up a lunch of cheese and fruit when she saw Midge's blue Subaru pull up to her cottage.

Watson leaped onto the back of the couch, ears alert.

"Hoping for tunaroons?" Faith asked, giving him an affectionate pat on her way to the door.

Midge was wearing jeans and a geometrically patterned long-sleeve shirt. Her fingernails were painted fuchsia with tiny white flowers. Her green eyes were shadowed with concern. "I had to stop by before heading to the stables." She gave Faith a quick hug. "Are you okay?"

"I'm fine," Faith said, warmed by her friend's concern.

"Everyone's talking about you finding that artist right here on the grounds. It must have been shocking, honey." Midge studied her. "You seem peaked. Are you sure you're okay?"

"I'm sure," Faith said reassuringly. "I was just finishing lunch. Do you have time to join me for a cup of coffee?" Although it was a bright afternoon, the air was frigid. Hot coffee would help chase away the chill.

"Coffee sounds great. I was hoping you hadn't left for the library yet." She stooped to pet Watson, who had wrapped himself around her legs. "Now, Watson, I just brought you treats yesterday," she chided. "And here you are, buttering me up for more."

"He's insatiable where tunaroons are concerned," Faith said, taking Midge's arm and leading her into the kitchen. "But he deserves them. Poor Herbert might still be down in the Peter Pan fountain if Watson hadn't gone snooping and found him."

"I heard the police think it was murder."

Faith started a pot of coffee. "The investigation is just getting started, so they don't have any answers yet."

"Who could have done such a thing?" Midge sat down at the table. "Do you think it was someone here at the retreat?"

"There are some possible suspects. The police have been taking statements from everyone connected with him—his wife, his former partner, a few other writers and artists who knew him. But it could have been someone from the outside who knew he was going to be here. Like I said, it's very early in the investigation."

"I heard it was his own weapon and everyone thought it was rubber or plastic or something. Imagine him having a real cutlass with him. What was he doing in that pirate getup anyway?"

Faith poured two cups of coffee and carried them to the table. "It was part of his exhibit—only he couldn't find his portfolio when it was time to set it up. That's the last time any of us saw him. Tuesday. I didn't find him until Wednesday after the evening program and refreshments."

"Katrina wasn't too cooperative when we asked about her husband yesterday afternoon," Midge mused, then took a sip of coffee. "She practically slammed the door in our faces."

"The chief said Katrina was pretty broken up when she got the news from Officer Rooney last night. They didn't appear to be the most devoted couple, but it must be awful for something like that to happen to the man you married. I mean, they must have loved each other once."

"I imagine," Midge agreed, not sounding convinced.

"Wolfe wants us to extend every courtesy to her," Faith said, sipping her coffee reflectively. She tapped a finger on the mug. She did feel sorry for Katrina, but it was also possible that she might tell her something that could shed some light on what happened. Or reveal some clue that she was guilty. "Perhaps I'll go up to her suite this morning to offer my condolences."

"Do you want some company?" Midge asked, peering at Faith over the rim of her coffee cup.

"I was hoping you'd ask," Faith said. "Do you have time?"

"There's nothing too pressing at the stables—just a routine check on the horses to make sure they're ready for Saturday's sleigh ride. Any word on Mrs. Tompkins's Chihuahua?"

"Mouse seemed much better when we were all summoned to the library last night. He still shivers, but his eyes looked less weepy."

"Good." Midge took her cup to the sink and rinsed it. "Come on. You can ride in my chariot."

Faith wrapped up a strawberry strudel she'd bought at Snickerdoodles. She hoped it would remind Katrina enough of her homeland to be considered a gesture of goodwill.

She left Watson to soak up the sun on the back of the couch. "I'll be back for you later," she said, ignoring his decidedly peeved expression.

When Faith and Midge arrived at the manor, they found a somewhat subdued atmosphere. It wasn't surprising, given what had happened. It was a relatively quiet time with guests taking a break after lunch.

"Have you seen the exhibit?" she asked Midge as they approached the library.

"No, but I'd love to take a peek. Mrs. Tompkins was telling me about her book."

"*Bailey the Bastille Mouse*," Faith supplied with a smile. "Maud is anxious to see what Mr. Delacroix makes of it. I think it's adorable, on top of being a clever way to expose kids to some history."

"Well, look at that!" Midge exclaimed as she perused the colorful exhibit. "I'm not partial to vermin, but that little guy is just darling. Mrs. Tompkins is certainly gifted."

"She is," Faith agreed, noticing that the table formerly reserved for Herbert Grissom had indeed been removed and the gap closed. She glanced down the row of tables and saw the plaque with Kip Rudyard's name on it.

The man himself loitered over it as though admiring his own handiwork. Then he turned and saw her. "Ah, if it isn't Marian the librarian," he said, heading in their direction.

"Faith Newberry," she corrected, trying to keep the annoyance out of her voice. "How are you today?"

Kip snorted. "Thanks to Grisly Grissom, we're all locked up here like prisoners and being given the third degree. So I'm not exactly a happy camper."

Had the man never heard it was poor form to speak ill of the dead? She swallowed her dislike of the stocky man whose pale eyes always seemed to be intruding and ignored his rude remark. "You may not have met Castleton's concierge veterinarian. This is my friend Midge Foster." She turned to Midge with a guarded look. "Midge, this is Rupert Rudyard."

"Please call me Kip," he said. "Glad to meet you. But I don't suppose I'll be needing your services since I left my old hunting hound, Bud, at home. More's the pity."

"Well, good luck with your exhibit," Faith told Kip, then took Midge's arm and propelled her down the row.

When they were out of earshot, Midge released her breath. "Who was that?"

"A frustrated illustrator," Faith said, "and he's obviously not a fan of Herbert."

"He's a fool to make that known," Midge said. "Do you think he's the one who—you know?"

"He might be. Scary, isn't it?" Faith shuddered and turned toward the staircase. "We'd better look in on Katrina."

Midge's step faltered slightly, and her shoulders straightened when she saw someone descending the stairs.

Léon Delacroix, dressed casually in gray pants and a white cable-knit sweater, carried a charcoal flannel coat. A crimson scarf hung loosely around his neck.

"Is he the one you were telling me about?" Midge whispered as she regarded the tall, silver-haired man.

There was no time to respond, for he stopped at the base of the stairs, evidently waiting for them to approach. "Good afternoon," he said with a slight bow.

"Hello, Mr. Delacroix."

"Leo. Just Leo, remember?" A humorous glint lit his dark eyes.

"Leo," Faith repeated obediently. "I'd like you to meet Midge Foster. She's my good friend and our concierge veterinarian, and she also has a very successful pet bakery in town."

Leo took the hand Midge extended and lifted it to his lips. "It's a pleasure to meet you," he said.

"And you," Midge said with a slight stammer.

"Leo Delacroix is our special guest for the retreat," Faith explained, amused by his effect on the women around her. "He represents Maple Publishing in Quebec."

"I see you are meeting our fine concierge veterinarian." Marlene approached the little group by the staircase and focused on Leo. She wore a gray pencil skirt topped by a turquoise blouse. Every blonde hair of her coiffure was perfectly in place.

Leo turned to Marlene and nodded.

"Is there anything I can get for you?" Marlene asked him. "I see you're about to go out. Can we have your car brought around?" The assistant manager virtually stumbled over herself in her effort to accommodate Leo.

"Thank you, Ms. Russell," Leo said. "I'm simply going out for a breath of fresh air. I'm in need of nothing." He inclined his head politely. "You've thoroughly seen to all my needs."

Marlene took a step back. "I'm glad to hear it. In that case, I should check on plans for tonight's event. I'll just toddle along." And she disappeared down the hall.

Toddle? Marlene never says "toddle." It was all Faith could do not to giggle.

"Ms. Russell is quite efficient, isn't she?" Leo commented. "I was told she would be extremely attentive—and indeed she is." He gave another slight bow and said to Faith, "I hope you are recovering from your unfortunate experience last night. Too bad about Herbie."

"Thank you," she said awkwardly. It seemed a rather inadequate remark where death was concerned. And yet, he was trying to be kind, wasn't he?

A shadow seemed to darken his eyes even further. "I'm sorry. A most regrettable occurrence."

Faith nodded.

Midge appeared slightly uncomfortable and said nothing.

As though sensing their tension, he smiled broadly. "I wonder if I might persuade you to accompany me to the play later this evening. It would be a delight to have two such lovely ladies on my arms."

A gala evening at the local playhouse had already been planned for the retreat guests. The variety event was composed of Christmas music, dancing, and short vignettes that showed off the talents of local musicians and even a couple of professionals.

Faith was glad for the outing because it would give the guests the opportunity to get away from the manor and forget about yesterday's shocking event for a little while.

"I couldn't possibly. My husband, Peter, and I have a dinner engagement with friends." Midge smiled at Leo. "But I do thank you for thinking to include me."

Leo turned to Faith. "And you? We're all going as a group, of course, but it would give me much pleasure if I could escort you." He winked at her. "Otherwise, I'm afraid I'll be left to the considerable wiles of Patsy O'Neil."

There was no rancor in the comment, yet Faith thought it sounded a little rude. To be fair, Patsy's behavior was overattentive where Leo was concerned. It seemed that every female at the manor was in some measure bewitched by him. And he definitely seemed to enjoy it.

Originally, Faith had planned to attend the event along with the guests, but since Herbert's murder, she'd hoped to spend a quiet night at home with Watson. "Well, things have been somewhat unsettled . . ." Her voice trailed off.

"All the more reason for you to enjoy yourself," he wheedled. "I could meet you at the library at seven thirty, and we can join the group at the theater."

She laughed. "You're very persuasive. Are all French Canadians that way?"

"No, I'm one of a kind," he said with a smile.

With all the commotion over Herbert's death, there had been little time to pay attention to their guest from Quebec. The least Faith could do was see that Leo had a good time at the play. It would be safe enough, and Marlene, who had planned to shuttle the entire group in special coaches, would approve of her attentiveness to the manor's special guest.

Faith hoped so. She would still rather be curled up at home tonight.

"I'll be at the library by seven thirty," Faith answered, hoping her reluctance didn't show.

"I will see you then." Leo bowed, then strode away.

"Enjoy your walk," Faith called after him. She tucked one hand in Midge's elbow and carried the strudel in the other as they climbed the stairs.

"He's quite the charmer," Midge said when they arrived on the second floor, where the guest suites were located. A few seconds later, she added, "At least on the surface, so you'd better watch out."

Faith laughed. "I'll watch it. He is a bit too smooth, isn't he?"

"Remind me. Which suite is Herbert's wife staying in?" Midge asked, glancing down the corridor.

Faith stopped dead in her tracks. Something clicked when she heard the artist's name. Had Leo referred to Herbert as Herbie? The only person who had used that name was Herbert's wife. Had Leo been acquainted with the artist? *This might be worth investigating.*

Midge turned to Faith. "Are you okay?"

"I'm fine. She's in the Robert Louis Stevenson Suite." Faith ushered her friend to the door and knocked.

There was no response.

Faith knocked louder. "Mrs. Grissom?"

There was a muffled sound inside, then the piercing squawk of Herbert's parrot.

The door opened, and Katrina stood there in a blue silk blouse and black pants. Her blonde hair hung unbraided to her shoulders, and there were dark circles under her eyes. "*Ja*, what is it?"

Faith was momentarily speechless. She had expected to perhaps see Katrina mourning quietly in her room. But the woman seemed almost frightened and wound tighter than a drum.

"Leaf new!" the parrot screamed from his cage. "Pity more!"

Katrina put her hands over her ears and muttered something in German.

Finally, Harley went quiet except for the sounds of his scratching on the cage and shaking his water dish.

"I'm sorry. We didn't mean to bother you, Mrs. Grissom," Faith said. "We thought you might enjoy this strudel from the bakery in town." She held it up and entered the suite.

Katrina didn't object, so Faith took the opportunity to scan the room. The contents of a few suitcases were sprawled on the bed, and drawers in the oak desk near the window were partly open, papers half in and half out—many strewn on the floor. Nearby, a fire in the hearth blazed. Had Katrina been feeding something into the flames?

It appeared that Katrina had been searching for something. Or was she preparing to leave the manor?

Midge followed Faith inside and asked Katrina, "Is there anything we can do for you?"

"Since you will be staying here for the time being anyway," Faith added with emphasis. She couldn't imagine that Katrina would ignore the police order and try to leave town.

"Yes, you can get rid of that bird and leave me in peace," Katrina said bitterly. "I've told the police everything, and I have nothing more to say." She wrapped her arms in front of her as though to ward off an invasion.

Given the tragic circumstances, she had a reason to be unfriendly—and afraid, Faith supposed. But it seemed that it would be in the woman's best interests to act civil to a staff member of the manor where she was currently residing. And did she really expect someone else to assume responsibility for her husband's parrot?

Faith cleared her throat. "We're not here to cause you any further distress. As representatives of Castleton Manor, Midge and I simply want to—"

Suddenly Katrina burst into tears. She covered her face with her hands and backed into a chair near the door.

"Pity!" Harley ranted. "More's the pity!"

Faith gave Midge a sidelong glance, then closed the door.

Midge wandered over to the parrot, making soothing sounds and inspecting the bird's cage.

Faith retrieved a box of tissues from a nearby table and handed it to Katrina when the woman's sobs began to subside.

The woman blew her nose loudly and peered up through her fingers.

Faith wondered if Katrina was trying to gauge how her visitors were reacting. Were her tears genuine or staged for their benefit?

Katrina blew her nose once more. "I didn't kill my husband!" she cried, shaking her disheveled hair.

"Where were you when he disappeared?" Faith asked.

"I was shopping, like I told you, and I thought he had gone off the way he often did." Katrina shook her head. "He was a difficult man. He always said things will be different. He will turn over a new leaf. But it is always the same."

"New leaf!" the parrot screamed. "New leaf, me hearty!"

Katrina put her hands over her ears. "He said to Harley, 'I'm turning over a new leaf,' and now the bird says the words over and over. Who can stand such noise? It makes me crazy. But Herbie only laughed at me. I didn't get along with him lately, but I could never kill him. I told the police so."

"Were you aware that the cutlass your husband wore as part of his costume was a real weapon?" Faith asked.

"*Ach nein.* I don't touch Herbie's costumes. They were special to him. Someone must have put that thing there. Maybe whoever killed him."

Harley squawked and pecked at the bars of his cage.

"The police should find that man who killed my husband and leave me alone. I want to go home." Katrina broke into a fresh bout of tears.

A childish reaction, Faith thought. But under the circumstances and considering Katrina probably had no family apart from whoever might be left in Germany, she could be forgiven. The widow admitted that she did not get along with her husband, but she must have cared for him.

And if Harley made that much noise all the time, Faith felt that her own nerves would probably be pretty frayed too.

Midge walked over to Katrina and put a hand on her shoulder. "Would you like me to take Harley to the kennels until you feel a little stronger?" she asked gently. "The staff will take good care of him."

Katrina gave Midge an appreciative glance. "Yes, *bitte*. I do not want him here. He was Herbie's pet. He does not like me."

"Pity! Pity!" the bird squawked. "More's the pity!"

Faith was suddenly brought up short. Green-winged macaws like Harley were known to speak, and this one uttered silly words and meaningless phrases.

But what if those mimicked phrases weren't as meaningless as she assumed?

What if they could provide a clue to his master's death?

11

Faith settled herself at her desk in the library. She had fed Watson and got ready early so she would have time to search the Web before meeting Leo and the other guests for the evening at the playhouse. She was wearing a black dress, and she hoped Leo didn't assume she had dressed up for his benefit.

She assumed it would be easy enough to dig up background on Herbert Grissom, though certainly the police had already done careful vetting, including bank records and holdings. It hadn't taken them long to discover the couple's life insurance situation. She didn't know if she'd be able to discover anything else, but she had to try.

Social media turned up nothing of real interest. The information in Herbert's profile contained only the basics, such as his enrollment at the School of Visual Arts in New York City and the fact he'd earned a degree from Columbia University. There was nothing of a personal nature. She couldn't even find a reference to Katrina.

Then Faith researched the publisher for the Perry and the Pirate series, but that didn't turn up anything useful either.

She sighed and drummed her fingers on the desk. Could Katrina have killed her husband? Probably not. The stabbing had been so forceful that it was likely beyond the woman's strength.

Then Faith thought of Katrina's obvious searching for something in the suite she had shared with Herbert and the fireplace blazing in the middle of the day, in spite of the more than sufficient heat in the manor. What had she been up to?

Faith decided it was worth informing Chief Garris, so she called him.

Though it was after usual business hours, the chief answered almost immediately.

She told him what she had seen a few hours earlier. "It may mean nothing, but I thought you should know. Katrina seems all over the place emotionally. One minute she's belligerent, and the next she's breaking down in tears."

"Emotional instability is a pretty typical response to the death of a spouse," the chief said. "We don't have enough to charge her, but we're discreetly watching her."

Faith wasn't surprised that the police were keeping tabs on Katrina. Especially tonight because the widow had opted to stay at the manor. Katrina had claimed that she had a migraine and she was going straight to bed.

"We have impounded Mr. Grissom's car, so she can't just take off. And we have also seized her passport." Garris was quiet for a few seconds. Then, as though thinking out loud, he said, "We've searched every inch of her suite at the manor and her home in New York as well. We've discovered nothing incriminating."

Faith frowned. *Back to square one.*

"However, we did find a curious detail that might be relevant. About ten years ago, Mr. Grissom made an unusually large deposit in payment for his artwork. The money was immediately funneled into an offshore account. But details of the deposit have been lost, and we've been unable to locate the agent who brokered the deal."

"Does Katrina know anything about it?"

"She claims no knowledge of the money," the chief answered. "It happened about six years before they were married."

Faith sighed. Even if the money had something to do with Herbert's death, it sounded like the police had run into a brick wall. They might never know for sure.

"I don't want you getting involved in this case," Garris said suddenly. "If Mrs. Grissom is guilty, she could be dangerous."

She thought of the hostility in the woman's eyes. Had Katrina hated her husband enough to kill him? Today she had seemed more frightened than anything.

Faith went on to talk about stopping in with Midge to see Katrina. "It was only a social call to see if we could help. When Katrina admitted the parrot was driving her crazy, Midge offered to take him off her hands. The bird is staying in the kennels for now, but eventually we'll have to figure out what to do with him."

"Let me know if you think of anything else that might be important," Chief Garris said.

After promising to be careful and to call with any further information, she disconnected.

Faith heard guests gathering in the hall outside the library. Leo would be waiting.

When she emerged from the library, she saw Leo waiting a short distance away. He was surrounded by several guests who all vied for his attention, including Patsy.

As soon as Leo noticed Faith, he broke away from the guests. "You've been working," he said as though Faith had been caught in some minor deception. "All work and no play, you know. But don't you look marvelous." He cast an admiring glance over her outfit and added, "*Vous êtes radieuse.*"

When Faith caught herself smiling, she realized she was not immune to his charm. "Thank you."

Marlene appeared and started herding the guests to the door so they could board the buses that were to convey them to the theater. The assistant manager had ordered two luxury coaches, equipped with every convenience and comfort.

"They're calling for us to board. Shall we?" Leo said, extending his elbow.

Faith tucked her hand into the crook of his arm and walked with him to the door.

It was a gorgeous starlit night, the air crisp and clear. Snow draped the grounds like an ermine stole—seamless and thick. Evergreens rimmed the distant hills, and only the very top of the Peter Pan fountain could be seen, the hedge forming a discreet curtain around it.

It was hard to imagine that anything macabre had occurred anywhere on the manor's beautiful acreage.

The guests took seats in the buses amid happy chatter.

Leo led Faith toward the back of the first coach. He ushered her into a seat by the window, then took the seat beside her.

Across the aisle, Felix sat alone in the window seat, staring out into the darkness.

She studied his profile, the thin blond hair that touched the collar of his charcoal overcoat. *A loner*, she mused, recalling that she hadn't seen him converse with anyone since that first evening when he and Herbert had argued.

The motor hummed. They were about to head out when the door opened again, admitting a last-minute boarder.

Wolfe stepped up into the coach, checked his watch, and surveyed the passengers. He spotted Faith and nodded.

She smiled, acknowledging his unspoken greeting.

Then Wolfe glanced at Leo, and something flashed across his features.

What was in his expression? Surprise? Disapproval? Surely not jealousy. Faith pushed away the ridiculous thought.

Wolfe said something to the driver and sat down behind him in the first row—the seat obviously reserved for him as host.

Now Faith could see only his back, elegant in his black wool coat and scarf, dark hair shining in the overhead light.

"I guess we're on our way," Leo said, jolting her out of her reverie. "Are you looking forward to this holiday concert as much as I am? I mean, it's good to have a pleasant evening away after all the trouble Herbie caused."

Faith sucked in a breath. Other guests called him Herbert. Kip, who had also chosen to remain at the manor tonight, had dubbed him "Grisly Grissom." Only his wife called him Herbie. But Leo had now employed the nickname once more. Again, Faith wondered if Leo had known Herbert.

He shrugged and spread his hands. "Well, *c'est la vie*."

That's life? Faith squelched a quick retort. Was Leo really that cavalier? A man was dead.

Her body language must have shown her feelings, for Leo turned toward her and added apologetically, "I don't mean to sound harsh, but from everything I've heard he was a most disagreeable man and probably brought the trouble on himself."

With a calmness she was far from feeling, she asked, "Were you acquainted with Mr. Grissom? I've heard you refer to him as Herbie twice now."

"I have not had the dubious pleasure," Leo responded. "Obviously, I must have heard someone else call him Herbie. That was his name, wasn't it?"

"I thought you might have met him through your publishing circles," Faith persisted. "The adventure series he illustrated was quite popular a couple of years ago, and his work is excellent."

"Though I'm not acquainted with it—or the man—I'm sure it is as you say," he said with deliberate emphasis and an ingratiating smile.

Faith recalled the moment she'd discovered Herbert silenced and alone in the snow. "It's such a waste," she said, sighing. "Who knows what he could have gone on to do?"

Leo remained quiet for so long that Faith turned to him. In profile, he appeared suddenly changed—almost a stranger.

He narrowed his eyes as though he were staring down a long tunnel, then released a breath. "Indeed," he said so quietly she had to lean closer to hear. Then he gazed beyond her. "Have you ever lost someone very close to you?"

Faith immediately thought of her maternal grandmother, whose death had nearly unhinged her. Finding Watson and nursing him back to health had helped her heal. "Yes," she whispered. "It's so hard."

"You know it happens," Leo said, still apparently lost in that nostalgic fog. "Death. But when it grabs you by the throat, you never quite throw off its ugly hand. It clings to you, and it tightens around you until—" He stopped, as though suddenly waking from a bad dream. "Forgive me. This is supposed to be a gala evening, and here I am talking about something as unpleasant as death."

Faith was a bit startled by his reaction. She wanted to say she was sorry for whatever memory had clearly disturbed him. "There's nothing to forgive. This tragic event has us all a little off-balance."

As suddenly as his somber mood had come over him, it vanished. "So, tell me, do the police have any idea what happened to him?" he asked with a note of concern in his voice, the first she'd heard from him.

"He was killed with that cutlass he was wearing, and someone else was definitely involved. They will find out who it was, of course. In the meantime, it's just awful that it has happened—and that someone attending this retreat or even someone who works at the manor—"

"Or lives in Lighthouse Bay," Leo added, raising silvery eyebrows. "But my money is on his wife. I'm betting she couldn't take it anymore."

"Katrina was away shopping during the time her husband was missing and insists she's innocent," Faith said, mulling over the alibi. "She has also been visibly distraught since it happened. She was in such a nervous state that she couldn't stand the constant squawking of her husband's parrot."

"I find pet birds obnoxious," Leo scoffed. "I can't believe the man brought a parrot to this magnificent mansion."

"That shouldn't be so surprising," she said. "A lot of our guests bring pets with them. Mrs. Tompkins always has her little Chihuahua, Mr. Watkins has his labradoodle, Ms. O'Neil has her Pekingese, and surely you remember my Watson."

"Yes, of course," he said.

"Are you allergic to birds? This could be a long retreat if you are." Faith grinned at the look of horror on his face. "Don't worry. The parrot is being kept away from the guests because he was quite disruptive." Impulsively, she said, "Actually, I'm adopting him temporarily."

Leo laughed. "You are enjoying the subtle art of humor at my expense, are you not?"

"I'm terribly sorry," Faith said. "I promise to be nice the rest of the evening."

They arrived at the playhouse, and the burden of conversation was suspended as they all disembarked from the buses and took their seats inside.

The concert was completely entertaining, and Faith was able to stop thinking about the murder for its duration. There were comic vignettes and a rendering of "Baby, It's Cold Outside," featuring a glamorous diva and a handsome off-Broadway star brought in for the evening. The guest soloist sang many familiar and inspirational songs of the season, including "Ave Maria," which always left Faith with a deep sense of awe.

During the brief intermission in the lobby, she broke away from Leo and the guests who were doing their best to capture his attention.

Patsy, who had managed to snag a seat on Leo's other side during the concert, kept close at his elbow, whispering to him frequently.

Faith spotted Marlene and crossed the room to join her. "I think everyone is enjoying the evening."

"That's good," Marlene said distractedly, casting a glance in Leo's direction.

Faith realized that Marlene would far rather join the little group clustered around Leo than be charged with hosting the guests and making sure everything went well. Somehow Marlene hadn't even been able to finagle a spot for herself on the same coach as the retreat's special guest.

Before Faith could say anything else to Marlene, one of the guests approached and pulled the assistant manager aside.

Faith glanced around. She noticed Felix perusing playbills in a glass case. Though his hairline was receding, he had the appearance of youth and good health. *Clean-cut* was the description that came to mind. Almost too clean. Could this loner have committed murder with his old partner's sharp sword?

She walked over to him. "Are you enjoying the concert, Mr. Anderson?" she asked.

"Yes. It's a good performance," he answered, stepping back slightly and turning toward her.

They were about equal in height, so Faith could look directly into his blue-gray eyes. They reminded her of a clouded sky, and they were soulful and arresting.

"It's good of you all to make such excellent arrangements for us," he remarked.

"I'm glad you're enjoying yourself," she said. "I couldn't help but overhear you and Mr. Grissom the other night, and I had to tell Chief Garris about your argument. I'm sorry if it made things difficult for you."

Felix blinked and seemed startled for a moment. Then he passed a hand lightly over his jaw. "It's all right. It's no secret that we worked together—quite successfully at first. The police would have dug up our entire working relationship rather quickly without your assistance."

"What happened?" Faith asked, emboldened by his calm attitude. "Perry and the Pirate is a wonderful series. Kids couldn't get enough of it."

A nostalgic look passed over his features. "It was something I'd always wanted to write—since I was a kid myself. I was never the strong, adventurous type, but I wanted to be. I guess I put all my thwarted desire into my character."

Faith gave an understanding nod.

"Perry must have been believable," Felix continued, "because kids believed him, and they can't be fooled, you know. In the end, they always know. Herbert captured Perry perfectly. Kudgen the pirate too. It was almost magical—well, at least it was for a while."

When a long moment passed, Faith urged, "What happened?"

"I was fired," he said simply.

"Why?"

"Herbert said he was going to find a new writer for his characters." A small bitter laugh escaped his lips. "Turn over a new leaf or something like that."

"His characters?" Faith asked, confused. "But I thought you created them."

"I did. But Herbert began demanding to speak for Perry—especially Perry. And he wanted to change his appearance—make his character harder, tougher. It was all wrong. He was transforming the character into something petty and dangerous. Someone children couldn't—shouldn't—believe in."

"That's terrible," she said.

Felix let his breath out in a slow wheeze. "Herbert's dishonesty with the publishers and the outlets that moved the books was bad enough, but what he was doing to Perry—I couldn't stand for it."

"What happened?"

He shook his head slowly. "When I wouldn't go along with his schemes and his ideas about changing the stories, he fired me. From my own story! He threatened me with a huge lawsuit over rights to the books, and I don't have the money for something like that. So I just had to stop writing, at least until another idea came along."

"I'm sorry," Faith said. "It must have made you very angry."

"Enough to kill him? Is that your question, Miss Newberry?" His eyes darkened. It appeared a storm was brewing, but then it swiftly blew over. "I suppose I could have killed him. I was that devastated. But I didn't."

"Why did you come to this retreat?" Faith asked. "Did you know Herbert would be here too?"

"I didn't know, and when I found out I thought I could handle his anger. We're both professionals. Surely we could coexist for a few days. Or maybe I wanted to show him it didn't matter, that I was a bigger, stronger person and I was above resentment." Felix laughed. "I even thought, 'What would Perry do?' But it's been too long since I wrote him. I couldn't answer the question."

Before Faith could figure out what to say, the lights flashed, signaling to the crowd that the next half of the show was about to start.

"Nice talking with you," the despondent writer told her. He turned and headed back into the theater.

Faith went inside and reclaimed her seat. She was glad for the semidarkness of the theater. All the better for reflecting on what Felix had said. She was relieved that Leo didn't have a lot to say. He kept his focus on the stage, now and then deflecting a comment from Patsy.

On the ride back to the manor, Leo remained mostly quiet.

Faith responded to the few remarks he did make, but she forgot them almost immediately.

Mercifully, they soon arrived at the manor. As Faith walked down the aisle to depart the coach, she chided herself for being such unpleasant company.

As soon as she left the bus, she noticed a police cruiser parked outside the entrance to the manor. She gasped and rushed inside, pressing through the milling guests while scanning the foyer.

A woman screamed hysterically.

12

Faith glanced up to a small alcove in the foyer and spotted Katrina. Chief Garris was next to her, reaching out.

Faith hurried to the alcove, all her senses on high alert.

Katrina, her head in her hands, screamed again. She shivered in a thin lounging gown, long hair tumbling over her shoulders, and started to cry.

Faith ran to Katrina and knelt beside her. She removed her coat and draped it over the grieving woman's shoulders.

At the same time, the French doors off the loggia opened and Kip burst through them. But not entirely under his own steam.

Behind him, Officer Bryan Laddy pinned one of Kip's arms behind his back. With his other hand, the officer gripped the collar of Kip's corduroy jacket. "I got him, Chief," Officer Laddy announced as he pushed Kip toward the alcove where Chief Garris, Faith, and Katrina were cloistered.

Wolfe and Marlene raced in.

"What's going on, Chief?" Wolfe asked.

"There's been an incident," Garris answered. "Mrs. Grissom says Mr. Rudyard broke into her room. I understand they're both guests of this retreat."

"I didn't break in," Kip said breathlessly. "She let me in."

Faith peered at Kip. The man had chosen not to attend the theater that evening, saying he was going to visit an uncle who lived on the Cape. So what was he doing at Katrina's door?

"I told him to get out, but he wouldn't go!" Katrina wailed through her tears.

"It's not what you think. It's all a big mistake," Kip argued, his face flushed to a deep crimson. His jacket was torn, and the tails of his shirt hung over his pants, which were wet at the ankles—no doubt from running in the snow.

Officer Laddy steered Kip to a nearby chair. "Sit down. We'll get to you in a minute."

Garris addressed Wolfe. "One of your other guests heard the commotion and phoned it in. Because we were in the area doing surveillance, we were able to get here right away."

Remembering what the chief had told her about their surveillance of Herbert's wife, Faith wasn't surprised.

Guests started gathering, obviously trying to find out what was going on.

"I suggest we talk privately," Wolfe said to the chief.

"You can use my office," Marlene offered.

"Thank you," Wolfe said. Turning to the group of guests, he said soothingly, "Please allow us some privacy and return to your rooms. The situation is being taken care of."

Marlene began herding the guests away.

Wolfe caught Faith's eye. "I think it would be a good idea for you to come along with Mrs. Grissom if you don't mind." He paused as the guests cleared the area, then signaled for the group clustered in the alcove. "Please follow me."

Wolfe led them to Marlene's office in the basement and seated Katrina and Faith on one side of the desk and Officer Laddy and Kip on the other.

The chief stood next to Wolfe. He pulled a notepad and a pen from his pocket and proceeded to jot down notes.

"I don't know what all the fuss is about," Kip grumbled. "I merely wanted to talk to the lady and offer my condolences."

"This late in the evening?" Wolfe remarked, studying the man suspiciously.

"Didn't you say you were visiting someone this evening instead of going to the theater with the rest of the group?" Faith added.

"I did," Kip said impatiently. "I got back early and decided to drop by and see Katrina. After all, her husband and I were in the same artists group some years back. More's the pity. But I was just paying my respects, and she went crazy on me."

"Is that how you see it, Mrs. Grissom?" the chief asked.

Katrina's mouth worked, and she sniffled noisily. But the tears had stopped, and a sly triumph seemed to glint in her icy blue eyes. "He is *widerwärtig*."

Whatever that means, Faith thought, *it isn't a compliment.*

"He is not nice—not to Herbie either." Katrina raised her chin and tried to smooth her disheveled hair. "I told him to leave me alone."

Chief Garris glanced up from his notepad. "Did he threaten you? Did he hurt you?"

Katrina gave a grand shrug, knocking Faith's coat from her shoulders indignantly. "He would have if you had not come." She sniffed again and shielded her eyes with a hand.

Wolfe turned to Kip with a penetrating stare. "Why didn't you leave when she asked you to?"

"I was about to, but she kept ranting and raving at me. She was trying to embarrass me in front of everybody. I just . . ." Kip flung his beefy arms out in a gesture of frustration.

"But when I came after you, you ran away instead of stopping when I told you to," Officer Laddy added sternly.

"I didn't realize you were a cop. It was nothing, I tell you," Kip whined. "Whoever called the cops got it all wrong. I wasn't doing anything. I certainly wasn't going to hurt her."

"The person who reported it did the right thing," the chief broke in, clearly disgusted with the whole affair. "You two were carrying on, disturbing everyone's peace while Mr. Jaxon and his staff were away."

Faith knew there were other staff members in-house, but the guest who had called the police probably hadn't known that. It wasn't good for the police to show up at Castleton Manor. Marlene was most likely livid.

The chief turned to Katrina. "Do you intend to press charges?"

Kip's face paled, and he clutched the arms of his chair.

Faith noticed a poignant, threatening look pass between him and Katrina, as though a line had been drawn in the sand that neither wanted to cross.

Startled, Faith watched and waited. There had to be more to this strange situation.

"Mrs. Grissom, do you want this man arrested?" the chief said.

Katrina sat up straighter in her chair and squared her shoulders. "*Nein*," she said dismissively. "But he must not come near me again. I want to be left alone. Can not a grieving woman be left in peace to mourn her wonderful husband?"

Faith couldn't believe it. One minute Katrina admitted that she hadn't gotten along with Herbert, and the next she was mourning the loss and calling him wonderful.

From the expression on the chief's face, Faith knew he was having doubts about Katrina's state of mind too.

"I don't need to remind any of you that there is a murder investigation going on here," Chief Garris said darkly. "There's enough stress without this kind of childish behavior taking up our time and energy. I will have more to say to you soon, Mr. Rudyard. And don't even think about going anywhere." The chief motioned to Officer Laddy, and the two of them left with a nod to Wolfe.

"Faith, will you see Mrs. Grissom to her room?" Wolfe asked, detaining Kip with a hand on the big man's arm. "I'd like to talk to Mr. Rudyard here."

"I can find my room," Katrina said petulantly, not bothering to pick up Faith's coat, which she had carelessly let fall to the floor.

Wolfe reached for it and held it out to Faith while giving Katrina a stern look. "Please allow Miss Newberry to accompany you." With a meaningful glance to Faith, he escorted Kip away.

Faith ushered Katrina to her suite and followed the woman

inside. It was eerily quiet now that Herbert and his boisterous pet parrot were gone.

"Really, I am all right now. I am tired," Katrina said through chattering teeth. "You do not need to trouble yourself." Then suddenly she seemed vulnerable again, her face ashen, her hands trembling.

"You've had a grueling experience. I think you need a cup of tea," Faith said firmly. "I'll fix one for you while you change into something warm and get ready for bed."

"You do not have to," Katrina argued. But then she seemed to wilt. "Perhaps tea would be good." She turned and walked unsteadily into the bathroom.

Moments later, Faith heard the shower running.

She found an electric kettle on the marble counter and located an assortment of tea arranged in a decorative basket, along with packets of sugar and cream. In one of the cherrywood cabinets she found bone china cups and linen napkins. The Jaxon family spared no expense when it came to their guests' comfort.

When the kettle clicked off and the tea tray was prepared, Katrina had yet to turn off the water in the shower.

Faith sat down at the small table within sight of the door. She expected Katrina to emerge with a return to her brooding disposition and insist on being left alone. Whether she'd express a modicum of gratitude for Faith's trouble before shooing her out the door was anyone's guess.

Temperamental, moody, inscrutable, Faith reflected. *All of the above and more. But a murderer?*

She studied the cloth set diagonally on the dark wood table. It was designed like a map with various points indicating possible routes to a mythical treasure. Had Katrina been after a different kind of treasure—the insurance money that would be hers now that her husband was dead?

Was it possible that Katrina and Kip were in on it together? Had they killed Herbert for the insurance money? But if so, why would they risk drawing attention to themselves? What was all the fracas about? A lovers' quarrel?

Faith recalled the scene in the exhibit hall when Herbert had told Kip he'd never make it in the art world because he had no talent. Maud had remarked that Kip was sour because he seemed to garner so little interest from publishers.

After all, her husband and I were in the same artists group some years back, Kip had admitted just a little while ago. He must have known Katrina then too. Had he really been expressing his condolences when he'd gone to her room? Faith highly doubted it. But what had he been doing there?

Her gaze drifted around the room and the part of the sitting area that she could see from her vantage point. Katrina was far from a fastidious housekeeper. Articles of clothing were draped over chairs, and newspapers and paperback books were scattered around, some even on the floor. How had she accrued such a mess in the few hours since the housekeeping staff had been in to clean the rooms that morning?

Faith spied a crumpled piece of paper that hadn't quite made it into the wastebasket and idly picked it up. She found herself opening it, pressing out the creases. The handwriting was small, sloppily scrawled in a masculine hand.

Curiosity killed the cat, her brain chided, but she couldn't stop herself from reading it.

Hand it over tonight or I tell them!

She felt herself go rigid. It was definitely a threat. Could the writer be Kip, who had been to Katrina's room? Had he broken in as Katrina claimed, or had she given him admittance? What had he wanted? And what would he tell if he didn't get it?

Before Faith could further contemplate the threatening note, Katrina walked out of the bathroom.

She wore a fluffy spa robe, her hair wrapped in a white turban. She stopped short when she saw what Faith was holding. "What are you doing?" she screamed. Red-faced, she charged at Faith and snatched the paper from her hand.

Faith folded her hands and stared into Katrina's face. "I think I'm realizing that you didn't tell the truth to Chief Garris tonight. What was it Mr. Rudyard wanted from you when he came to your room tonight?"

"Nothing. It is nothing! You pick up trash from my room. You have no right." Katrina collapsed into a chair. And again, she became a blubbering child, fat tears spurting from her eyes and rolling over her crimson cheeks.

"What did you tell Kip?"

"I told him I do not know where it is," Katrina admitted. "I looked all through Herbie's things. I did not find what he wants."

Faith studied the distraught woman. Quietly, she asked, "What does he want?"

"Kip wants a letter from some literary agent. A letter saying he is a thief. He took credit for some paintings that were not his."

Faith was startled. She hadn't expected something like this. "How did Herbert get the letter?"

"I do not know. It was long before I know Herbie, but Herbie always held it over the man's head." She stared down at her lap. "He made him give money to be quiet."

Herbert had been blackmailing Kip? Faith's mind raced, recalling the scene between the two of them in the exhibit hall. She remembered the sneering words and the way Herbert had tapped the spot on his chest where a pocket might be as he claimed that Kip had no real talent of his own.

"Do you know how long your husband was taking Kip's money?" Faith asked.

"Kip said several years. Several thousand dollars." Katrina shrugged. "But I do not know if he is telling the truth."

"So you can't find the letter?"

"I searched everywhere, but I could not find it," Katrina repeated, shaking her head. The turban had fallen, and her wet blonde hair streamed to her shoulders. "I do not even know if Herbie had such a letter. I never saw it."

Kip had to be in terror that the police might find the letter. *If it existed*, Faith thought. Blackmail was definitely a motive for murder. Did Kip kill Herbert to silence him? And was it true that Katrina didn't know where the letter was? She had already proven that she could be dishonest, and to the police no less.

"Is that what you were doing the day we came for your husband's parrot?" The place had been a mess, and Faith had wondered at the time if Katrina was burning some sort of evidence in the fireplace.

Katrina nodded. "If I found it, I would burn it with Herbie's letters. I do not want money from Kip, and I do not want anything from the man I married. I burned his letters, letters saying how much he loved me, what a good life we would have. He said he was turning over a new leaf, and his new drawings would make us rich. I want only to forget." A fresh paroxysm of weeping overtook her.

The letter could mean more blackmail—this time from Herbert's wife—and had the potential to ruin Kip's chances of a publisher purchasing his work. When Faith had first shown Leo the exhibits, he'd seemed interested in Kip's illustrations of horses. It might be the frustrated artist's big break.

Faith decided she had no choice but to be blunt. "This is the time for truth. Did you kill your husband? Is that what Kip will tell if you don't give him the letter?"

"*Nein!*" Katrina shouted. "But the police think I did. And if they know that I was here—that I was out walking in the beautiful snow—they will put me in the jail!" Her eyes widened in terror.

Katrina was in a country not her own, her husband was dead, and she was under suspicion for his murder. It was a heavy load, and the woman appeared to be breaking beneath the strain. Faith couldn't help but feel sorry for her, though she still didn't know if she could trust her.

"The best thing is to tell the truth," Faith said. "Yes, you have motive and opportunity, but you haven't been proven guilty. You haven't even been arrested."

Katrina sniffed and wrapped her arms around herself as though to get warm. "I did not kill Herbie," she said again. "I think it was Kip Rudyard."

"If he did it, the police will find out." Faith stood, wishing the whole mess were over. "Tomorrow you should go see Chief Garris. You must tell him what you've told me."

"Why are you helping me?" Katrina asked, furrowing her brow.

Faith felt a pang of sympathy. Had Katrina been so bereft of kindness? Of friendship? Did she have anyone to help her through this tragedy? "Surely you want to find out what happened to your husband," she said gently.

Katrina didn't respond. She only stared at Faith through reddened eyes, clearly still puzzled. She looked small and fragile in the chair, like a deflated balloon.

"Drink your tea and try to get some rest." Faith patted the woman's drooping shoulder on her way out the door.

Suddenly bone-tired, Faith descended the staircase and left the manor.

As she trudged home through the gardens, she considered the missing letter. It was obvious that Kip was jealous of Herbert's success. And to make it even worse, Herbert had been blackmailing Kip, and his shot at a successful career was now in jeopardy.

Had Kip finally decided enough was enough? Was he the one who had permanently silenced the abrasive illustrator?

13

Friday morning, Faith woke up groggy and wished she could linger in her serene little cottage.

Watson studiously ignored her, even when she put kibble in his bowl.

Poor Watson. She'd left him on his own a lot with the strange goings-on at the retreat, not wanting to put him in potential danger. She added a tunaroon to his breakfast, but he didn't budge from his perch on the back of the couch. She really was in the doghouse.

"Would you like to go to town?" she asked him.

The cat jumped off the couch and raced to the door.

Faith laughed. "I hope that means you've forgiven me."

The manor's library wasn't scheduled to open until after the first round of morning classes that day, so Faith drove to the Candle House Library for an emergency meeting of the book club. She needed her friends' sympathetic ears and wise advice.

They were already waiting when she flung herself through the door and breathed in the atmosphere that meant friendship and safety to her.

Watson was at her heels. When he strolled into the room, he pointedly avoided Atticus and proceeded to curl up in front of the fireplace.

Midge's little Chihuahua gazed at the cat adoringly. He was ever hopeful of becoming Watson's friend one day.

Eileen pulled Faith into her arms. "You look terrible. After a gala evening at the playhouse—and with Léon Delacroix no less—I expected to find you beaming this morning."

Faith cast an accusing gaze at Midge. "Is nothing sacred?" she asked wryly.

Midge laughed, an amused twinkle in her eyes.

"The music was superb, but the evening was far from a gala," Faith insisted. "And I wasn't *with* Léon Delacroix. I merely agreed to accompany him—like the loyal employee I am."

Brooke helped Faith out of her coat. "Everyone's talking about the police grabbing Kip Rudyard for breaking into Katrina Grissom's suite."

"What are you doing here?" Faith asked, startled to see her.

Brooke smiled. "Angelina told me she could handle lunch prep for an hour or so. When she's at work, she is absolutely invaluable."

"Let's have some refreshments before we dive into business." Eileen indicated the brownies and a pot of dark roast coffee on a nearby table.

The women helped themselves, then got comfortable in the cozy reading chairs clustered around the fireplace.

Atticus jumped onto Midge's lap, and Watson remained in front of the fireplace.

"Kip didn't exactly break in," Faith said, taking a sip of coffee. She recounted what had happened and how Katrina had finally admitted what Kip wanted.

"Herbert was blackmailing that Kip Rudyard fellow?" Eileen asked incredulously.

"For several years—and several thousand dollars. At least that's what Kip told Katrina, but she doesn't know for sure."

"What did Herbert use to blackmail him?" Midge asked as she straightened Atticus's festive green-and-red bow tie.

"It was a letter from a literary agent saying that Kip had taken credit for paintings that weren't his," Faith explained. "It could destroy his chances of publishing his artwork. Herbert baited him at the literary exhibit, threatening to make his plagiarism known at the retreat."

"Does Katrina have the letter?" Eileen asked.

"She doesn't seem to. When Kip confronted her about the letter, she said she didn't know where it was," Faith answered. "But he didn't believe her. He threatened to tell the police that he had seen Katrina walking on the grounds during the time of her husband's death."

Midge raised her eyebrows. "Do you think Kip killed Herbert for the letter?"

"Or do you think Katrina killed him for the insurance money?" Brooke proposed.

Midge groaned. "It sounds like a case of he said, she said."

"I'm sure Katrina and Kip were both questioned thoroughly," Faith said, "but obviously no arrest has been made yet. The police must not have any solid proof that either is guilty."

"I did some checking on Kip," Eileen piped up.

"What did you find out?" Faith asked.

"I learned he's into building," Eileen replied. "He seems to be moderately successful at buying old houses and fixing them up himself. He must be quite handy with a hammer and a saw."

"Well, he has the muscles for it," Midge remarked. "He likes to show them off. Along with his tattoo."

"Half the population has tattoos these days," Brooke said. "I went out with a guy once who had a snake on his bicep. When he flexed his muscles, the reptile looked like it was alive and ready to spring." She shuddered. "It gave Diva and Bling the creeps too."

The other women laughed.

"What more do you know about Kip?" Eileen asked.

"His parents were Irish immigrants who made their lives here but weren't able to leave much to their kids," Faith replied. "He says he's a frustrated illustrator, and he tipped his hand early on that he resented Herbert's success."

"First blackmail and now jealousy," Midge said. "Kip certainly has strong motives."

"Anything else you can tell us about Kip?" Eileen persisted.

"Maud Tompkins knows him," Faith answered. "She says he makes the rounds of a lot of events in hopes of selling his illustrations, sadly without success. More's the pity." She gave a wry grin. "That seems to be his favorite phrase."

Suddenly, something clicked in her brain. *Pity! Pity! More's the pity!* They were the words she'd heard Harley the parrot shriek when he wasn't squawking like a feathered banshee.

"It's a weird phrase," Midge observed. "Nobody says it anymore, do they?"

No, Faith thought, *no one but Harley and Kip.*

Midge looked at her strangely, obviously waiting for a response.

Faith pressed her fingers to her temples. "Do you remember when Katrina complained about Harley, and we took the parrot out of the Robert Louis Stevenson Suite at her request?"

"Yes," Midge said slowly. "That bird was so noisy. But he wasn't just screaming. He was talking, wasn't he? And I believe one of that bird's crazy phrases was 'More's the pity.' Or sometimes just 'Pity.'"

"Kip must have been in that suite before—or at least been around the parrot often enough for the bird to mimic his words." Faith glanced at each of her friends. "I wonder what else Harley might have to say."

"Parrots are extremely intelligent," Midge said. "A green-winged macaw can be taught any number of tricks if he's happy and well-fed. They're good talkers." She paused. "I bet that bird knows a lot more than anyone thinks."

"Exactly," Faith said. "Do you want to come with me to the kennels? I want to adopt Harley for a few days, but I have no idea how to care for him. That bird might just shed some light on what happened to his master."

"Sure. But how do you think Watson will react?" Midge asked.

Upon hearing his name, Watson stopped grooming himself and stared at them.

Faith took a deep breath and let it out slowly, remembering the natural antipathy the cat had shown for Harley—even through glass.

She addressed her cat. "I'm going to owe you a ton of tunaroons for this assault on your dignity."

When the brief meeting of the Candle House Book Club ended, Faith and Midge arranged to meet at the kennels.

"But first I'm going to drop Watson off at home." Faith knew he would have a hard time adjusting to their new houseguest, and she didn't want to force him to ride in the car with the parrot too.

After leaving a sulky Watson at the cottage, Faith arrived at the kennels. Midge was already waiting for her.

The kennels were designated for the care and keeping of the resident animals. Guests could also board their companions there, though most people kept their pets with them in the manor. The immaculate kennels provided every luxury for the pampered pet.

Faith especially loved seeing the horses that roamed the paddock on winter mornings and stayed warm and comfortable in the stables at night.

It was one of Watson's favorite haunts too—for obvious reasons.

Even before they entered the kennel office, Faith heard Harley's shrill cries.

She and Midge exchanged glances.

"Are you sure you're ready for this?" Midge asked.

"No," Faith said honestly. "But I don't know if I have a choice. I need to find out if Harley can give me some answers."

Annie Jennings, a young kennel attendant, stepped outside and greeted them warmly.

Faith returned her infectious grin. She liked Annie, with her thick brown hair and her large hazel eyes over a spray of freckles.

Annie had been raised in upstate New York, but she was partial to cowboy boots and spurs. She had married a rancher quite a few years her senior. They raised horses and Angora goats together, and they seemed to be the quintessential happy couple.

"Harley doesn't squawk all the time, does he?" Faith asked Annie.

"Not all the time. But let's say a good portion of it, bless his heart." Annie tossed her thick braid over her shoulder. She loved all kinds of animals. Even the annoying ones. "I have a goat at home who hollers even more than he does."

"Well, we're going to give you some relief from the noise for a while," Midge told her. "Faith wants to take him to her cottage. She thinks the administration will agree. As for the owner by default, she doesn't care one way or the other what happens to Harley."

"Sounds good." Annie slipped her hands into the pockets of her jeans. "I was sorry to hear about Mr. Grissom. It's just awful. Did they catch the killer yet?"

"The police are still investigating," Faith said. "Has Harley said anything? I mean, apart from squawking most of the time?"

"Nope," Annie said, "but green-winged macaws don't talk when they're uncomfortable or lonely. It's my guess that being surrounded by strange animals in here stresses him out, and he probably misses his owner. I hear Mr. Grissom was quite a character. He dressed like a pirate and even talked like one. Downright strange."

"Can we see him?" Faith asked.

"Sure. Come on back."

Inside the kennels, they passed a poodle and a dachshund tugging a shaggy rope between them, growling playfully. An older dog, whose playful days seemed to be behind him, lounged nearby as if refereeing the match.

Annie stopped in front of Harley's roomy cage. "Here he is. He's beautiful, isn't he? Even though he can be noisy, I'd love to have him myself."

Harley was undeniably a handsome specimen, fully thirty-five inches long. The parrot sat quite still on his perch made from a tree branch, as if sizing them up even as they examined him. His head, shoulders, and breast were a vibrant red. The green band below the shoulders that gave his species their name yielded to bright blue on his wing tips. The bird's long, tapering red tail feathers were tipped in blue as well.

"Hello, Harley," Faith said, taking only one step toward the cage and keeping her voice low.

The bird shuffled farther down his perch as he surveyed the visitors. His upper beak was horn colored with dark gray on the lower sides—a formidable beak that could probably crack a finger with ease. Harley began chewing on the branch, stopping every few seconds to stare at them, but he made no sound.

"What does Harley eat?" Faith asked.

"Wild green-winged macaws eat a variety of seeds, nuts, fruits, and vegetation," Midge answered, "but you'll need commercially prepared seed or pellet mixes."

"You can have the supply we ordered for him. He seems to like it okay," Annie offered, digging into a cabinet.

"If you run out, I carry the pellet mixes in my shop, and I can order more for you," Midge said. "He can also eat anything healthy that you eat. Make sure he gets some protein. They usually like chicken, but keep him away from chocolate and avocado. They're poisonous for him."

"Thanks. I'll depend on your expertise to keep him well-fed and happy," Faith said. "I'll talk to him as much as I can and listen to the words he already knows."

"New leaf!" Harley screamed suddenly, spreading and fluttering his wings. "Turn over! Turn over!"

"It's all right, Harley," Faith said soothingly, glancing at Midge for support. "Watson and I will take good care of you." *Odd*, she thought. *"Turn over" was something you might say to a dog you were trying to train.*

As though understanding that he was about to become a roommate to a cat, the parrot screamed louder, tossing his head.

"He hasn't been out much today," Annie said apologetically. "A large macaw like Harley needs at least an hour outside the cage every day. Two or three hours would be better."

Harley shrieked again.

Faith groaned. Parrot-sitting was going to take some getting used to—and she didn't even want to think what Watson would have to say about the matter.

They picked up Harley, cage and all, and went outside. Mercifully, the bird was quiet—likely because Annie had drawn his night sheet over the cage.

"He'll be fine," Annie assured Faith. "You have a way with animals."

"Can you manage without me?" Midge asked. "I should check on the horses and get back to my shop."

Faith nodded. "Thanks for your help. And yours too, Annie."

Midge waved, then walked to her vehicle.

"By the way," Annie said, "are there any kids staying at the manor right now?"

Faith thought a moment and shook her head. "Not unless the Jaxon family has arrived. They always come for Christmas, but I haven't seen them yet. Why do you ask?"

"Late last night, the guy who's been taking the night shift heard a noise behind the kennels," Annie said. "He went to investigate but didn't see anyone. It was probably only the wind knocking against the shingles. But I thought I'd ask."

"Why did you think it was kids?"

"I found a bit of chocolate wrapper back there this morning." Annie removed a wadded piece of paper from her jeans pocket and held it up. "Our staff is usually careful about keeping the grounds neat. We must have missed this one." She stuffed the wrapper back into her pocket.

"It does sound strange," Faith agreed.

"Have fun with Harley. Let me know when you want to bring

him back." Annie smiled. "Not everyone is willing to put up with his noise for long."

Faith said goodbye, then loaded up the bird in his cage and drove off toward her cottage. "If I can manage to keep the peace between him and Watson," she said under her breath, "Harley's noise might just be very useful."

The cat ate what was left in his dish and carefully washed his face before leaping up onto the back of the couch. It had been warmed by the sun, and he padded to the far end to sprawl in his favorite spot.

His human had dropped him off, and he was feeling neglected. Why did she leave him here? He would enjoy spying on the humans who came into the large room with all the books. He could get out if he wanted to, and he often had, but a cat got tired of having to escape all the time. He'd like to be invited for once.

The last time he'd been at the manor, many of the humans had stared at the big tree that had somehow gotten inside. They had put all kinds of bright trinkets into its branches. When his human wasn't paying attention, he'd sniffed and pawed them just enough to see them jiggle. What fun—especially when they twinkled and sparkled in the light—but he'd be in big trouble if he knocked one off.

Maybe he had broken one, and that was why he was being ignored. But what good was a tree you couldn't climb and baubles you couldn't bat around? And why bring it inside if you were only going to gawk at it?

He snoozed awhile, and when he woke up, he noticed the sun had moved farther away. There was almost no warmth left on the couch. He felt himself getting more and more vexed. He was bored.

The cat sat up and peered through the big picture window. Nothing was going on. There wasn't even a squirrel to watch. He liked to pretend he was a great hunter, ready to spring. He could bring home a prize for his human. While she praised him, he would sit demurely and pretend it was nothing.

But there was no human to praise him. Maybe he'd sneak out now and see what his person was doing at the manor.

He was about to jump down from the couch when his human's car suddenly appeared.

At last! Maybe she had brought something for him—a treat or a new toy he could ignore until her back was turned.

He felt a purr coming on, even though he planned to snub her when she walked in the door.

But what was this? His human was pulling something big out of the car—something wider than she was.

He perked up his ears. What was that screeching?

Oh no, not the nasty bird that had knocked him off his comfortable seat in his human's car. She was bringing it to his sanctuary—opening the door with one hand and struggling to get inside with the thing.

How could she? He darted under the couch.

The parrot screamed when his human swept the covering off the thing that resembled a house with bars. It ruffled its wings, sending bits of red and green feathers flying.

"There, there, Harley," his human said in her best placating voice. "You're all right. You're safe here." She carried his funny house to a table by the big window and set it down.

The bird was not far from where the cat had been sitting in the sun only moments ago. Right next to his favorite place.

He gave a low growl.

"Come on out, Rumpy. It's all right." His human got down on her knees and reached for him. "Harley needs someone to take care of him, and you and I are going to do it—just for a little while."

Not only had she brought home that screaming bird with the puffed-out chest and wicked-looking beak, but she had called him by that name in front of that loathsome creature. She could call him from now until suppertime, but he wouldn't move an inch. Well, maybe an inch, just to have a look at that green monster.

Dark times had descended. He huddled under the couch, resolved to stay there as long as the bird was in the house.

14

The next morning dawned with crystal brilliance. The sun draped the white landscape with dramatic shadow and light.

Faith felt a sense of relief. Watson's first night with Harley in the cottage had proved uneventful, largely because Watson had maintained his distance, glowering at the bird through watchful green slits.

For his part, Harley had been subdued, occasionally pecking at food and water dishes and preening his feathers. He had uttered only a few grunts and clicks as he cocked his head.

Faith had spent a long time with the bird before covering his cage for the night. She wondered about the relationship between man and beast. Did Harley mourn for his dead master? Had Herbert been kind to him? Would the bird trust the strange woman who had temporarily taken him in?

Her thoughts turned to the day ahead. It would be particularly busy because the children were scheduled to visit Castleton Manor this afternoon. The manor staff were determined to make it a joyous experience for retreat guests and the young visitors. She hoped the sponsors would follow the directions to avoid the area where the crime had occurred. Faith looked forward to the event with equal doses of happy anticipation and dread.

Eager to get to the library, Faith got ready early. She fed Watson and ate her own breakfast, then carted him off with her to the manor. She didn't have the heart to leave him with Harley. She felt guilty about leaving the bird alone so soon after he'd lost his owner, but at least her cottage was more peaceful than the kennels.

She was surprised to see someone jogging on the plowed walkways not far from her cottage. It was rare in heavy snow to see a guest running for exercise, but the man she spied some fifty yards away moved with easy grace, as though it were a warm spring morning.

She trudged on toward the mansion, aware that whoever the hardy athlete was, he would soon overtake her.

"Good morning!"

Faith turned as she recognized the voice.

Leo Delacroix loped along easily in a dark running suit with thin crimson stripes on the pant legs and sleeves.

She shouldn't have been surprised by his vigor and lithe athleticism. It was obvious from his physique that he didn't spend all his time in the business world of books and publishing.

He whipped off a woolen hat to reveal flattened silver hair. His face was pink from the wind and cold, making his eyes flash like dark jewels.

"Good morning to you," she replied cheerfully. She felt vaguely embarrassed. When she had noticed the police parked at the manor after their trip to the theater, she'd taken off without a word and hadn't spoken to him since. "I didn't know you were a runner."

"It's good for the body and the mind," he said heartily without straining for breath. He smiled at her, his teeth gleaming in his flushed face. "Are librarians always up this early?"

"Sometimes," she said. "There's a lot going on today."

"A lot has been happening, that's for sure," he said, arching his brows. "And you've been in the thick of it. I understand you're quite a clever hand at solving mysteries. Something of an amateur sleuth."

"I wouldn't go that far," Faith replied. She gestured to the cat trotting beside them. "Watson's the canny one."

He studied her. "Are you all right? I saw you with that Grissom woman—Katrina, isn't it?"

Faith cringed. Was Leo pumping her for information? There was a good deal of talk among the guests, and she didn't want to add to the gossip. "I'm fine," she said with as much optimism as she could muster.

"It was a misunderstanding between Mrs. Grissom and Mr. Rudyard. It's over, and she's doing all right."

Desperate to change the subject, she continued, "I hope you've made some good contacts for your subsidiary company. There are many talented writers and artists attending the retreat. Three of them will read their stories for the children later today after the sleigh ride."

"Ah yes," Leo said, "the sleigh ride. What a charming idea. My compliments to the planning committee."

They arrived at the main entrance of the manor, and Leo reached for the door before Faith could open it. He stood back to usher her and Watson inside with a grand gesture. "Well, I'm glad you're all right. You and Mr. Watson here."

"It's Watson. Just Watson," she corrected with a smile.

Leo laughed.

The cat didn't linger any longer. He bounded inside.

Leo touched her arm lightly. "I wanted to thank you for coming to the play, but I'm sorry the night ended so abruptly."

"I'm sorry too. I mean, everything kind of came to a screeching halt. I didn't mean to be so rude."

"Not at all," he replied gallantly. He bowed as though to kiss her hand again.

But Faith moved away quickly, calling over her shoulder, "I hope you enjoyed your run."

When Faith arrived at the library, Watson was already waiting for her, with the air of one who would be tapping his foot impatiently if he had the ability. He scooted inside as soon as she opened the door.

She hung up her coat, and Watson curled up in a chair in front of the fireplace. She went over and stroked his sleek black fur from head to arched back.

She wouldn't have to open the library for a little while, so she decided to stop by the salon. She was eager for coffee and one of Brooke's breakfast scones.

"Be a good boy while I'm gone," Faith told Watson. She left him napping in the chair.

In the salon, a few guests were clustered at the round tables, sipping coffee and chatting amiably. Not gossiping, Faith hoped—but then, who could stop the curious mind?

She waved to Maud, who sat across from a woman with white hair and busy hands. Naomi Bender, a grandmother from Iowa who personally painted the illustrations for her stories about cats, was relating an entertaining story, judging by Maud's delighted laughter. Faith was glad to see her new friend enjoying herself.

Felix sat near the back of the room. He wore a cable-knit sweater over casual pants. Resting his arms on the table, hands folded in a contemplative gesture, he spoke with a woman sitting on the edge of her chair with her back to Faith.

Felix's companion was slender and small with dark hair drawn into a chignon at the back of her head. She leaned forward as Felix spoke to her.

Faith was glad to see Felix with a companion. He usually sat alone and walked alone, and he didn't even have a pet for company, at least not with him. Retreats such as this one could foster friendships, some that continued long after the event ended. In fact, she knew several guests who had made such friendships at annual conferences and now attended them together year after year.

Perhaps some hurt of the past shadowed Felix, making it difficult for him to connect with other people. Faith felt sorry for him, for that haunting melancholy in his eyes.

Brooke entered, carrying a tray of fresh scones. She wore a white apron over her pink blouse and gray slacks, somehow managing to look fresh and perfect, though she had already been working for a good three hours that morning.

Faith caught her eye and motioned to an empty corner table.

"Morning," Brooke said brightly, setting the plate down in the middle of the table. She took a seat across from Faith. "I've asked Angelina to make a fresh pot of caramel mocha and bring it in when it's ready. How does that sound?"

"Delectable," Faith murmured. "I didn't make coffee before leaving the cottage this morning, so I'm definitely ready." She sighed, adding, "Long night."

"Did Harley keep you awake?" Brooke asked, blue eyes twinkling with mischief.

"Actually, he was pretty quiet. So was Watson. He's not exactly happy with me or with Harley, but I think he'll come around. And Harley, I hope, will make himself useful too."

Brooke scanned the room and pursed her lips. "I don't quite know what's come over her," she said in a low voice.

Faith followed her gaze to the table where Felix sat.

The woman with the dark hair rose suddenly and crossed the room, leaving Felix staring after her with his sad eyes.

Faith was about to ask who Brooke was talking about when she realized the woman was Angelina Cordova, Kevin's mother, who had all but collapsed when she was summoned to take a bow for her dessert at the banquet.

"Angelina?" Faith whispered.

"Yes, she never wanted to leave the kitchen, never wanted anything to do with anyone, and now . . ." Brooke shrugged. "Well, she must be feeling better to interact with guests of the retreat." She pushed her chair back and stood. "Angelina!" she called.

The petite woman turned and obediently approached Brooke. She wore an apron too. Faith hadn't noticed it before. The blue cotton dress beneath it flared gracefully from a slender waist and fell just below her knees.

Angelina drew her brows together. "Oh, the special coffee!" she exclaimed. "I'm sure it's ready now. I'll get it."

She turned to go, but Brooke reached out and caught Angelina's arm. "It can wait. I'd like you to meet my friend—the librarian I was telling you about. This is Faith Newberry. She met your son the other day. His librarian friend, Eileen Piper, is Faith's aunt."

Faith extended a hand. "Hello, Angelina."

"I'm pleased to meet you," Angelina said, her hand small and cool in Faith's grasp. "Brooke talks about you all the time."

"Nothing bad, I hope," Faith joked.

Angelina smiled. "Of course not. And Kevin loves your aunt. She is good to him."

"Will Kevin be here for the sleigh ride this afternoon?" Faith asked, remembering that Eileen had said he would probably be coming. He was not among the homeless or in-transition, but Eileen had invited him personally, knowing he and his mother had a hard time making ends meet.

Angelina nodded, her eyes lighting at the mention of her son. "Yes. It is kind of Mr. Jaxon to let him and the other children come." She glanced at Brooke and took a step back. "I will get the caramel mocha now." She turned and hurried away.

Faith wondered why the shy Angelina had been sitting with the equally reserved artist Felix. And what had passed between them just before she had suddenly left him at the table?

Was it possible they had known each other before the retreat?

And if so, had their meeting just now been deliberately arranged?

Faith spent the morning in the library, helping retreat guests locate books and reference materials that interested them and catching up with necessary paperwork. In addition, she prepared the library for the story-reading segment of the children's Christmas party, which was scheduled to take place after the sleigh ride and right before dinner.

Watson accompanied Faith to the cottage for lunch. She decided it would be best to leave him there when she went back to the manor for the party. To make up for it, she gave him a few tunaroons, hoping they would keep him busy enough that he didn't mind his unwanted roommate so much.

The cat accepted the treats as his due and began to savor one of them.

"You two be good while I'm gone," Faith told Watson and Harley.

The parrot had been quiet since she'd walked in. Now he squawked, "Turn over! Turn over!"

Watson gave her a petulant look before she closed the door and left.

When Faith returned to the manor, the air was charged with anticipation. It was almost possible to forget that there had been a murder at Castleton, that someone among the staff or guests might be responsible. Almost.

The bus carrying twenty-four children, Eileen, and two other sponsors pulled up to the manor at one o'clock. The kids poured out of the vehicle with excited chatter. Wide-eyed wonder shone on their small faces as they gazed around at the beautiful snow-covered grounds and the three charming horse-drawn sleighs awaiting their arrival.

Carriages had been cleverly adapted to resemble real sleighs, complete with jingling bells. Faith had seen the stable staff working on them all week, but she still didn't know how they had managed to pull off the transformation.

Wolfe, Marlene, and the rest of the staff welcomed the children, giving out scarves, hats, and mittens for those who hadn't brought them. The guests of the retreat as well as staff members who could take a short reprieve from their duties had been invited to participate, and all were fully into the spirit of the afternoon.

When Eileen got off the bus, she walked over to where Faith stood. "They're so excited. I don't think any of these kids have been on a sleigh ride before."

Faith glanced at Kevin climbing up into the sleigh with his mother. His curly hair stuck out beneath his ski cap and obscured one large brown eye. Angelina appeared young and vibrant in a blue stocking cap and muffler.

"I'm glad Angelina came too," Faith said. "She hasn't wanted to join in any activities until now."

Then Felix stepped onto the sleigh and found a seat next to Angelina.

Faith was surprised at the sight. Had these two introverted individuals found a kindred spirit in each other?

Or was it something more sinister? Faith shook her head, pushing away the absurd notion. She didn't want to imagine that the two might have known each other previously and purposely arranged to meet at the manor for some kind of mischief.

When the sleigh was nearly full, leaving only the front row, Eileen announced, "Time for us to get on board too. Come on, Faith."

They climbed onto the sleigh and sat down. Behind them three rows of eager children bounced and squealed.

"Is there room for one more?" asked a deep voice.

Faith turned to see Leo. He was clad in a fleece jacket and the same woolen hat he had worn earlier. He smiled at her hopefully.

"Certainly," Eileen said, scooting over to the left and gesturing for Faith to move over too.

Leo climbed up and slid in next to Faith.

The space was small—too small. They were shoulder to shoulder, thigh to thigh. She drew an uncomfortable breath. There was nothing to do. They were stuck for the thirty-minute sleigh ride.

Behind her, the children whooped and hollered.

Someone started singing "Jingle Bells," and they were off and running.

If there was a bright side, Faith supposed, it was that it was too noisy for conversation. Earlier when Faith had run into Leo, he had seemed much too eager for Castleton Manor gossip. She feared he would continue to press her for information. So she inched closer to Eileen, knowing she was cramping her space.

They glided over the snow, giving the Peter Pan fountain a wide berth. When Faith regarded it, she didn't detect even a hint that anything dark or scary had happened there. She was grateful that the police had released the scene in plenty of time for the manor staff to tend to it.

Now and then the driver would prod the horses into a quick trot, and the children would laugh and cheer.

When the ride was over—much too soon from the children's perspective—Leo gallantly helped the exhilarated children and guests down. In the process, he held Faith's hands somewhat longer than necessary before releasing her.

She wondered why she wasn't as taken with him as the other women at the retreat.

Fortunately, she had no time to stew on it. The children were being led into the library, where a warm fire burned in the grate.

It was story time.

The younger children settled down on the colorful Persian rug. Kevin and a few of the other older kids sat in the comfortable red couches brought close for the storytelling segment.

As planned earlier, the guests retrieved their pets and brought them to the library. Howard walked in with his gentle labradoodle, Bandit, trotting at his side. Patsy carried her longhaired Pekingese, Holly. And Maud cradled her tiny Chihuahua, Mouse.

The appearance of the dogs brought cries of delight from the children.

Fortunately, the three dogs seemed comfortable with small hands, and all the children were gentle with them. Mouse even settled in a little blonde girl's lap.

First, Naomi Bender read her story about Lang, a Siamese cat who belonged to a royal prince. The prince was a spoiled boy who mistreated Lang. Sometimes he forgot to feed the cat, and he left her out in a dark courtyard when he was angry with her. One day, Lang ran away and met a poor little girl who loved and cared for her for the rest of her life.

The kids sat entranced while Naomi read the tale, occasionally reacting to the story with a gasp at the prince's meanness or agreeing with how the poor girl cared for Lang.

When Naomi held up the book to show them her charming paintings, the children squealed with delight. They clapped loudly when she finished.

Maud's rendering of *Bailey the Bastille Mouse*, however, brought the house down. Her full-color illustrations showed the courageous mouse riding atop a banner carried by a young French boy leading the march against those who oppressed the common people.

The children pressed forward to get a better look at the drawings and cheered the courageous little mouse.

Faith scanned the crowd and noticed that Leo was listening and watching attentively. He was clearly impressed. She was happy for Maud, knowing the retired teacher possessed a worthy voice in the world of children's literature.

When Maud was finished, Mouse yipped and danced on his tiny paws as the children laughed and clapped.

Maud beamed as she watched them.

The lights began to dim for the reading of "'Twas the Night Before Christmas." Jessie Willcox Smith's illustrations from the 1912 edition of the book would be projected on the wall. It was the final presentation before the children would join the retreat guests in the grand banquet hall for dinner.

While the celebrated local storyteller was reading, Wolfe moved to the door that led to the foyer beyond the library.

Faith had noticed Wolfe standing with arms crossed, taking in the proceedings from the minute the children had returned from their sleigh ride, and wondered what he was thinking.

Now as he stood at the door, Faith could make out one of the staff members handing Wolfe a large package.

But there was no more time to wonder about a delivery important enough to interrupt the owner of Castleton Manor. The reading was over, and the children were being ushered to the banquet hall for dinner and a special dessert. Afterward, they would be treated to a visit from Santa.

Faith turned out the lights on the Christmas tree and prepared to join the party.

But Wolfe stopped her at the library door. "Please take a look at this," he said without preamble, his features somber, blue eyes clouded. He walked inside and set the large package on the table.

Faith followed. "What is it?" she asked.

Wolfe opened the package and removed a watercolor block. "I think these are Mr. Grissom's portfolio drawings."

"The ones he lost?" Faith asked.

"I believe so." Wolfe carefully turned the pages, showing her pastel renderings of a pirate wielding a cutlass and a young boy defying the marauding invader.

Faith stared in disbelief at the drawings of the boy. He appeared to be nine or ten years old, and he was thin and wiry. Dark, curly hair draped over his big brown eyes. He had a short nose and a small, round chin with a prominent dimple. The boy's arms were crossed in defiance, and his feet in unlaced tennis shoes were planted firmly on the deck of a pirate ship.

She felt her heart race. There was no doubt. She was looking at Kevin Cordova.

15

"What? How?" Faith gaped at the dark-haired boy in the drawings.

"One of the staff members went to empty the Dumpster outside and found the portfolio beneath it," Wolfe explained.

Faith's mind whirled. How had the pictures gotten there?

Wolfe slowly turned the pages. Some of the drawings were blurred and marred from days buried beneath melting snow and debris. "There's no signature anywhere on the drawings, but I still think this is the missing portfolio. This pirate bears an uncanny resemblance to Herbert Grissom."

"The boy looks just like Kevin," Faith blurted out.

"Kevin?" Wolfe ran a hand through his hair as he flipped back to the first page of the block and studied the drawing.

"Kevin Cordova," she said. "Angelina's son. She's the woman helping Brooke in the kitchen."

"Marlene said she had hired someone temporarily. Is Angelina the one who made such a hit with her dessert at the welcome banquet?"

Faith nodded. "Kevin's here today. Eileen knows him from the library and invited him. I met him the day Herbert's car bumped into mine. He was going to the library to get a book about hockey."

"I see," Wolfe said.

Faith peered more closely at the drawing of the young boy. At first, she thought there was no doubt it was Kevin. But now she second-guessed herself. Was she imagining the close resemblance? The way that lock of hair fell over his left eye, the light brown skin, the rounded chin with the distinctive dimple, the mouth tilted in an innocent expression? No, it was Kevin all right.

"But how?" she wondered aloud.

Wolfe flipped the large pages over, revealing more images in various poses—the boy pulling a chain attached to a golden chest gleaming with jewels, the boy tossing curly black hair in defiance with a rock in one hand. "Are you sure Kevin's the boy in these drawings?"

Faith tried to make sense of it. If Kevin had been the model for Herbert's drawings, it had to mean the artist knew him and likely Angelina too. She recalled seeing Herbert's car idling near the library when she'd first met him. His gaze had seemed to be trained on Kevin as the boy walked down the street. Had he been watching Kevin? "I-I think it is," she stammered.

"So Angelina must have known our murdered guest," Wolfe said. He stepped back, dropping the watercolor block onto the desk as though it might burn his fingers. "There will be prints on these drawings. We may be damaging evidence."

Faith's heart raced. "Do you think whoever stole the drawings might also have . . . ?" She couldn't finish the thought, seeing in her mind's eye a shy mother with large, dark eyes, who was even now helping Brooke serve the excited children in the banquet hall.

"The police will have to be notified," Wolfe said gravely. "And Angelina Cordova has quite a bit of explaining to do."

She couldn't have done it. Could she? Faith felt an icy shiver ripple through her. "Do we have to do it now?" she asked in a small voice. "She'll be helping Brooke, and her son is here."

"Maybe there's a reasonable explanation, but we do have to find out as soon as possible." Wolfe took out his phone. "I'll see if the chief is available to stop by and talk to her."

Faith sighed. Poor Angelina. Poor Kevin. How had it come to this? Felix Anderson, Kip Rudyard, and Katrina Grissom all had strong motives to do away with Herbert. But this gentle, hardworking single mother with her polite, hockey-loving son? Surely not.

Wolfe disengaged from the call and turned to Faith. "The chief will arrive in fifteen minutes. Please find Angelina and bring her back here."

"I'll bring Brooke too. Angelina trusts her. Maybe her presence will make it easier," she managed to say around the hard lump in her throat.

Wolfe nodded, his eyes warm with sympathy.

Faith left the library and plodded down the hall.

Laughter and happy chatter emanated from the banquet hall as she approached.

She quietly stepped inside the room and stood near the door. The tables were adorned with bright red cloths and sundae dishes that sparkled like crystal. At the center of each table was a miniature ceramic sleigh and reindeer on which Santa Claus sat, arm poised in the air as though wishing the world joy.

Dinner was obviously over already because the children were devouring ice-cream sundaes heaped high with whipped cream and multicolored sprinkles.

Mack, the maintenance man, would be preparing to make an appearance as Santa. Old and stoop-shouldered with a head of bushy white hair, he was a natural to play the part. He had worked at the manor longer than anyone else, and he was called on to repair everything from plumbing to vehicles.

Faith spotted Kevin sitting next to Eileen, who seemed to be enjoying the ice cream as much as the children were.

Angelina stood off to the side, smiling as she surveyed the scene. It pained Faith that the rare smile was about to be wiped away as she was interrogated for murder.

Who was this woman? What was she to Herbert Grissom? Faith remembered when Angelina had stepped out to receive the applause of the diners at the welcome banquet and then collapsed. Had she seen Herbert and recognized him? But why would she react so dramatically to his presence?

Brooke headed toward Faith. She was flushed and smiling.

Obviously, everything was going well. Faith didn't want to be the one to break the news to her friend.

"Eileen was looking for you. How about a sundae?" Brooke studied Faith. "What's wrong?"

"Wolfe needs to talk to Angelina," Faith said numbly. Her voice seemed to be coming from someone else.

A reflection of Faith's distress appeared in Brooke's expression. "Now?"

Faith nodded, the lump still lodged in her throat. "He's waiting in the library for Chief Garris to arrive. You should come too."

Brooke ushered Faith to the doorway, her voice hushed. "What happened? Why is the chief coming?"

Someone began the chorus of "Up on the Housetop." Faith knew it was Santa's cue to enter.

When Mack's practiced "Ho ho ho!" rang out, the room erupted with cheers.

Faith glanced into the room and watched the assigned elves file over to the giant Christmas tree lit with multicolored lights and ornaments. She returned her attention to Brooke. "Herbert's portfolio has been found."

"Where?"

"Under the Dumpster behind the manor," Faith answered. She didn't add that Angelina had easy access to that area. She could have quickly dumped the portfolio out there, and no one would have even noticed.

"What does the portfolio have to do with Angelina?" Brooke asked.

"Herbert's pirate drawings," Faith continued. "There's a young boy in almost every one of them. I recognized him immediately. It's Kevin."

"No," Brooke said, placing a hand on her chest. "Are you sure?"

"I wish I weren't."

"How can it be?"

"I don't know. Has Angelina ever talked about Kevin's father?" Faith saw in her mind's eye a sudden likeness between the boy and Herbert. The same dark eyes, the same curly hair, and the tilt of the mouth. Had a dimpled chin hidden underneath Herbert's bushy black beard?

"No. She said she's raising Kevin by herself."

Shouts of surprise and joy interrupted their conversation.

They turned to see the boys and girls opening their gifts.

Faith focused on Kevin. A long, ungainly box wrapped in bright red paper with a floppy green bow sat on the table in front of him. Kevin ripped off the paper, which Eileen took from his eager hands. The boy pulled out a black hockey stick with blue and white stripes on the upper half of the slender blade.

Eileen's face shone. Faith could tell that her aunt had known exactly what Kevin wanted and made sure his name was attached to the box containing the hockey stick.

There were tears in Angelina's brown eyes as she watched Kevin's stunned reaction, followed by unbridled delight.

Angelina took her son's hand—the one not clutching the stick—and walked with him to where Mack sat surrounded by his elves. It was clear they were expressing their thanks, as were the other children crowding around him. Angelina hugged her son before leaving the room.

When Brooke followed her assistant, Faith scooted inside and sat beside her aunt. She touched Eileen's arm and whispered, "Angelina was summoned to the library. She's going to be questioned by the police. She might know something about Herbert's death."

The glow of joy vanished from Eileen's face, but she quickly rallied. "I'm sure you'll tell me the whole story later. Kevin can come home with me until Angelina is free to pick him up. I'll tell him that she has to stay late to clean up after the party."

"Thank you," Faith whispered, giving her aunt a kiss on the cheek. She got up and hurried to the door.

Brooke and Angelina met her there, and they proceeded to the library together.

Faith didn't know what Brooke had told Angelina, but the woman seemed calm enough. Perhaps she was still glowing after witnessing the happiness on her son's face when he opened his gift.

The trio walked into the library.

Wolfe and Chief Garris were sitting at the table, and they stood when the women arrived.

"I'm Wolfe Jaxon, Ms. Cordova," he said, putting out his hand. "I own the manor, though Marlene and Brooke handled your application."

Angelina nodded.

Wolfe motioned to the table, where the portfolio was prominently displayed.

Angelina froze when she noticed the watercolor block of drawings. Her ashen face and rigid bearing removed any doubt that the portfolio meant something to her. She faltered.

Brooke put a steadying hand under her elbow.

"Please sit down," Wolfe said in a tone that was gentle but unyielding as he gestured to a chair at the table.

Faith and Brooke took the seats on either side of Angelina, and Chief Garris sat across from her.

"This is Chief Garris," Wolfe continued as he sat down beside the chief. "I believe you met him a few days ago."

The chief assumed an air of authority, but his voice was low and steady in the charged air. "Do you know why Mr. Jaxon brought you here?"

Angelina bit her trembling lip but said nothing.

"Do you recognize these drawings?" Garris reached for the watercolor block and slowly lifted the cover page.

Displayed in full color was the figure of the boy with the gently tilting mouth and curly hair flopping over his left eye.

Angelina slumped in her chair. She put her hands to her face, and her body began to shake.

No one moved or said a word.

Angelina seemed so upset that Faith longed to put her arms around her. Certainly this soft-spoken, gentle-eyed mother couldn't have committed so heinous an act as murder.

Could she?

"Ms. Cordova, where were you in the early hours of Wednesday morning?" the chief asked. "Specifically between one and three."

Angelina, hands still covering her face, shook her head. "I didn't kill him," she said in a voice so quiet Faith could barely hear her. "I didn't kill him," she repeated more firmly.

"Is this your son in the pictures, Ms. Cordova?" Garris said. "You need to tell us what it's all about."

Slowly, Angelina straightened. She lowered her hands and held them tightly in her lap. She kept her focus on the drawing and seemed to make a desperate effort to control herself. "I saw Herbert that night at the dinner. I couldn't believe it." She shook her head again as though to make the sight disappear. "He somehow found out Kevin and I were living here."

The chief removed a notepad and a pen from his front pocket. "What was your relationship to Herbert Grissom?"

As though she hadn't heard the question, Angelina continued with the same sad nostalgia. "It was so long ago. My brother and I moved across the country to Portland. We grew up in New England, but we had visited Oregon several times and liked it there, so we packed up and went. My brother got a job working for the shipbuilding company Herbert's family owned. Herbert worked there at the time. He was always interested in art, but it wasn't his career when I met him."

Angelina took a deep breath, as if mustering her courage to continue the story. "When my brother was killed in a storm at sea, I was completely alone." Her voice broke. "Herbert was kind to me. He let me work in the sail-making factory. He started coming to visit me, asking how I was doing, and eventually we eloped. We were truly happy for the first year or so. But after I had the baby, he changed."

"Herbert is Kevin's father?" Faith asked gently.

Angelina nodded.

"What happened then?" Garris prompted.

"He became cold and distant. He was trying to make a career with his art, and it wasn't going well. He started to take it out on me, and I knew I had to leave before he started turning that cruelty on my son. I got full custody of Kevin. Herbert didn't even want visitation rights."

"What did you do after that?" the chief asked.

"Kevin and I left Portland. I told Herbert we were going, which I had to do because we had a child together, but he didn't seem to care. I didn't want to see him again." Angelina lifted her chin. "I haven't seen him since. But then he found out I was in Lighthouse Bay. He told me he was sorry and asked to see Kevin. I said no." She gripped the arms of the chair. "No."

Faith leaned forward. What had led Herbert to seek out Angelina and Kevin after so many years? Hadn't Katrina said something about Herbert "turning over the new leaf"? Even Herbert had used the phrase when he was arguing with Felix before the welcome dinner. Her thoughts whirled. There were too many threads, and they seemed to become more tangled as the days passed.

"I need to ask you again," the chief said, "where were you during the time Herbert Grissom died?"

"I was at home with my son. I did not kill Herbert. Maybe I didn't want to see him again, but I did not kill him." Angelina wrapped her arms in front of her as though a bone-chilling cold had overtaken her.

"What about the drawings?" Garris asked Angelina, motioning to the portfolio. "Do you know anything about them?"

"I saw Herbert drawing my son. So I took the paintings and buried them under the big trash container. I did not want him to show them to the world and profit from them. Kevin and I have struggled for years without any help from him while he thrived. I didn't want him to use my son to get more success."

Chief Garris slid his notepad and pen into his pocket. He leaned back in his chair, his features somber.

Whether he believed Angelina or not, Faith couldn't tell. She couldn't even be sure of her own feelings. Could Angelina have been angry enough at Herbert for drawing her son to want him dead? And could she really attack him with a cutlass and leave him bleeding in the snow?

The chief stood and faced Angelina. "Is there anyone who saw you return home that evening? Did you happen to make any telephone calls during the night or go anywhere?"

Angelina shook her head. "No one saw me return, and my son and I were asleep all night."

The chief buttoned his coat and picked up the watercolor block. He nodded to Wolfe, then said to Angelina, "We'll want to speak with you again. Please stay in the area." And he left.

Faith checked her watch. It was late. The children had been taken home.

Brooke went to Angelina and touched her shoulder. "You should go home," she said gently. "Kevin is with Eileen, and he can stay with her tonight. You need to rest."

Faith expected the protective mother to refuse, but to her surprise, Angelina agreed. "That is so kind."

Either she's really tired or she really trusts Eileen. Or both.

"I am sorry for all this," Angelina told Brooke. "I do not blame you if you want to fire me now."

"I certainly don't," Brooke said adamantly. "You're a wonderful help in the kitchen. You've saved me more than once this week." She turned to Wolfe as if silently asking him to agree.

"There's no need for that, Ms. Cordova," Wolfe said. "Taking those paintings was wrong, but it is understandable. You are not under arrest, and Brooke needs your assistance in the kitchen."

"Thank you," Angelina murmured. "Thank you so much."

Faith was glad Angelina would not lose her job. Still, it would be difficult for her now that her personal life had been scrutinized, and it would continue to be investigated until the mystery of Herbert's death was solved.

Brooke helped Angelina to her feet. "I'll walk you to your car. In fact, I'll follow you home and stay over with you tonight."

The two said good night and left the library.

"I'll be going now too," Faith said as she began collecting her belongings.

"Let me see you to your cottage," Wolfe offered.

"It's not necessary," Faith said.

Wolfe smiled. "I insist."

"In that case, thank you," Faith said.

Wolfe's phone pinged. "Excuse me." He pulled it out of his pocket and checked the message.

Faith heard something at the door. Wolfe was still occupied on his phone, so she went to investigate.

She was surprised to see a man hurry down the hall. As the figure retreated, she caught a glimpse of gray trousers and a corduroy jacket.

The jacket seemed familiar. Had she seen it somewhere before? But where? And who? Kip Rudyard? He had a proven penchant for night forays and gossip. Had he been listening?

She chided herself for thinking that a grown man would be listening at the keyhole of the library.

Even so, she felt a shiver and was glad Wolfe had offered to walk her home.

16

The cat's ears twitched at the noise coming from the cage by the window. It was his window, where the sun made a cozy nest on the back of the couch. His window, where he could gaze out and see the squirrels scurrying across the snow and the winter birds scratching for food.

How dare this noisy pile of feathers usurp his window lookout where he watched for his human. Who, by the way, had been gone a long time.

The world outside the window was no longer golden with sunlight. Only a dim light in the black night filtered through the blinds to highlight the bird's beaky nose, the claws clutching the tree branch, and the ridiculous toys hanging on his cage.

The cat glowered as the parrot pecked at the bars and preened his feathers, puffing them out like a balloon.

One swirling feather wafted through the bars and tickled the cat's nose. How long must he endure this indignity?

The cat raised his head, sniffed at the feather, and turned his back to the bird. He swished his stub of a tail to show his disgust.

And yet, there was something about the way the creature stared at him with those wide red-rimmed eyes—like he had some great idea that nobody knew about.

The cat paced back and forth for a while, watching the bird and knowing that the bird watched him in return.

The bird screamed and rocked from side to side as though copying the cat's pacing.

Was the bird expressing a clumsy effort at play? The cat would choose when it was time to play. He glared at the cocked head—turning first right, then left, peering through the bars.

It must be awful to be stuck in there instead of riding on that big human's shoulder the way the bird used to.

Perhaps the bird was sad. It must be why the cat's human had adopted him. Alas, the cat would have to share his space now, but if he saw any tunaroons in that bird's cage, it would be no more Mr. Nice Cat.

He decided to take up a watchful post on the other end of the couch. It was as far away from the pest as he could get.

The bird screeched as the cat leaped up to his new post. Then he stopped and peered through beady eyes as though he heard something.

The cat perked up his ears. Someone was coming.

It didn't sound like his human. She made a great deal more noise when coming home. The cat heard clicking and scratching, then silence and more clicking.

A human opened the back door and a moment later entered the room. An unfamiliar human who didn't belong here.

The cat hissed to warn him away.

But the human seemed to take no notice. He went around the couch and reached out to the bird with something in his hand.

The bird scuttled to the back of his cage and batted his wings.

All the cat's protective instincts came to the fore. He sprang at the interloper, hissing and raking his claws across the human's neck.

"New leaf! Awk!" the bird shrieked, flapping his wings.

The human swiped at the cat, muffling his angry howls.

But the cat bit the hand that struck him and the foot that kicked at him. He struck out with his claws once more.

Clutching his face, the human sprinted out of the room.

The cat gave chase, but the person dashed out the back door.

When it was over, the cat and the bird regarded each other with newfound respect.

"I'm sorry you had to hang around so late tonight," Wolfe said as he stepped out of the library. "But I'm glad you and Brooke were here."

"Me too," Faith said.

The manor was quiet now, and there was no sign of the lingerer who had scuttled away.

Wolfe sighed and leaned against the door as though he wanted to prolong these few moments before venturing out into the cold. "It was an unfortunate way to end the Christmas party."

"The party was a success despite everything, though," she assured him. "You were good with Angelina. I mean, even though she caused some trouble, you were patient and kind." She couldn't think of a way to express how impressed she was by his efficient but compassionate handling of the upsetting evening.

"The woman's been through a lot," he said. "I can understand why she didn't want Mr. Grissom anywhere near her or her son."

"Kevin's a wonderful kid," Faith said. "I'm so glad he received the hockey stick he wanted. Leave it to Eileen to make sure Santa got it right."

They were both quiet for a long moment.

"She could have done it, you know," Wolfe said, raising his eyebrows. "And the chief is going to be thorough."

"He always is," Faith said in a small voice. "But she's not the only one with a reason to want Herbert dead."

Wolfe nodded. "Before you brought Angelina in, the chief told me that he questioned Mrs. Grissom about her husband's blackmail of Mr. Rudyard."

"Did he learn anything else?" Faith asked.

"I don't think so. The chief mentioned Mr. Rudyard's alibi checked out, but he's not completely off the hook just yet."

Faith shook her head, vexed at her own perplexity and unconvinced that any of them could be guilty. "I can't help but think we're missing something."

"It's best that we leave the investigation to the police. They're more than capable of handling the case." There was a warning in his piercing gaze.

She grinned at him. "Don't I always?"

Wolfe shook his head. "Come on. It's time to get you home." He chivalrously offered her his arm.

She took it, and together they headed for her cottage. As if by mutual consent, they took their time walking and didn't speak, allowing the serenity of the night to settle around them.

When they arrived at the cottage, Faith thanked Wolfe, and they said good night. He turned and headed back to the manor.

As Faith stepped inside the house, she felt a vague sense that something was amiss.

Before she could dwell on the feeling, she took in a surprising sight. Watson was perched on the back of the couch only a few feet from the parrot's cage on top of an end table. The two appeared to be the image of domestic tranquility.

"Well," she said, removing her coat and boots, "you two seem to be getting along."

Watson jumped down and twined around her ankles. Having company during long, lonely hours must have softened the cat's attitude. When his dinner was late in coming, he often gave her the cold shoulder.

After dishing out Watson's kibble, Faith returned to the living room, where Harley perched silently in his cage.

"What are all these feathers about?" she asked, picking off several from the couch and floor around the bird's cage. She wondered if parrots shed.

Then she realized the couch pillows were strewn untidily, and two were even on the floor. As she glanced around the room, she noticed a small, lightweight table was turned over.

"What have you been up to?" she asked Watson.

The cat blinked at her, then began washing his face. He was the picture of innocence.

While Faith righted the table, she spotted something small and dark on the floor near Harley's cage. It was a square of chocolate.

How did that get there? She must be getting careless in her housekeeping. She was a chocolate lover, so it wasn't unusual to find chocolate in the house. "But I seldom put it anywhere but in my mouth," she said to Watson.

The cat continued to wash his face.

Faith sat down on the couch, too weary to get ready for bed, though it was late. She brushed away a few more stray feathers and bits of food. Apparently Harley was a bit of a slob. Tomorrow she'd spread out some newspapers or a sheet beneath his cage.

The events of the long and eventful day whirled in her mind. She wondered what Angelina was feeling.

Angelina's story was sad, yet Faith couldn't help but feel sorry for Herbert Grissom too. Had he come to the manor's retreat because he wanted to connect with the son he had never known?

Harley began clicking his beak against the bars of his cage.

Faith turned to the bird. "You're a pretty boy, aren't you, Harley?"

"Pretty boy, aye, pretty boy!"

Faith was startled. He hadn't said much since she'd brought him to the cottage. Perhaps the bird was becoming less lonely for his lost master. "Harley, want a cracker?" she asked, instantly regretting the banality of the question. Why did people ask that question of every parrot who ever lived?

The parrot didn't respond.

"More's the pity," she said, testing the bird. "More's the pity!"

"Pity. More's the pity! Pity!"

Harley had probably picked up Kip's phrase. Maybe Kip had been with Herbert often. More likely, Herbert taunted Kip with the phrase and egged Harley on.

Then, remembering the other words she'd heard from Harley, she said, "Turn over a new leaf."

"Leaf! Leaf!" Harley screeched. "Turn over! Turn over! Awk! New leaf."

She knew that parrots often confused words and sounds. A friend of Faith's had once trained her parakeet to whistle "Yankee Doodle." He'd get part of the song right, then mix up the intervals. It had been a great source of entertainment.

Faith shook her head. What had Herbert meant by the phrase?

Katrina had told her that Herbert was always saying he was turning over a new leaf, and he claimed his new drawings would make them rich.

What did it mean? Probably nothing at all. It was crazy to think keeping Harley might help solve the riddle.

Faith got up and slipped the sheet over the cage. "Sleep well, me hearty," she told him with an ironic smile.

"Time for bed," she said to Watson, who had ceased his ablutions and sat observing her. "Come on. We'll make sure everything's locked up and call it a night."

She double-checked the front door, but when she got to the back door, she stood stock-still and sucked in a breath.

It was ajar.

She crept toward the door and inspected it. All around the casing by the exterior lock were new scratches. Not something made by a cat but by a two-legged creature and evidently with a screwdriver or another instrument.

Faith jumped back in alarm. Someone had broken into her cottage.

She reached for the dead bolt, first grabbing part of her shirt so as not to obscure any fingerprints that might be there. The upper lock turned easily. It hadn't been locked in the first place, but the bottom lock had been secured. The invader had picked the lock.

She stood at the door, willing her heartbeat to slow down. Why would someone want to get into her cottage? A thief? If someone was bent on stealing expensive artifacts or money, her house was the last place on the manor grounds the person would bother with.

So, what was the interloper searching for? She raced through the cottage, checking for anything missing. Her few jewelry pieces remained in their box in her bedroom, and the dresser drawers appeared undisturbed. Even the twenty-dollar bill she'd left on her dresser that morning was still there.

Faith returned to the living room, and Watson padded after her. She should call the police. But the chief had been at the manor late, and she hated to disturb him.

Nothing was missing, and she was fine—frazzled but fine. Tomorrow would be soon enough to dust the door and locks for fingerprints—assuming there were any besides her own.

She checked all the windows and the two doors, then turned the dead bolt on the back door. Satisfied everything was secure, she went back to the couch, all desire for sleep gone.

Faith pulled Watson onto her lap, felt the comforting warmth of his furry body. "Maybe I should have invested in a big dog instead of you," she teased the cat to lighten her fear.

His purr meant that he didn't take the comment seriously. As he shouldn't, because he had protected their home before.

There had been another time when a troubled young woman had broken into Faith's cottage and been scared away when Watson leaped down on her from the top of the fridge. She hadn't been able to explain the deep red scratches on her arms.

Faith lifted Watson's head and peered into his sleepy green eyes. "Were you playing lord of the manor again? Is there someone out there with telltale marks from your intrepid claws?"

17

Officer Jan Rooney pulled up to the cottage the next morning shortly after Faith's call to report the break-in. Faith was grateful that the officer had discreetly avoided the main house and employed no sirens.

Faith greeted Officer Rooney at the front door with a smile. "I'm sorry to bring you out so early in the morning."

She had phoned the chief at seven after a night when sounds had seemed amplified and unidentifiable. Even the murmurings of the ocean had failed to soothe her. Still, she had eventually fallen asleep with her cell phone at the ready and Watson snoring softly at her feet.

"It's not a problem," Officer Rooney said. "Let's take a peek at where the intruder came in."

Faith nodded and led her to the back door, where they stood outside in the frigid air.

The officer immediately began inspecting the nicks and scratches on the door without touching the area. She pulled out her dusting equipment. "Tell me what happened."

"I came home late," Faith explained. "When I went to the back door to make sure it was locked, I noticed it was ajar. Then I saw the scratches on the door and realized someone had broken in."

"And you say nothing is missing?" Officer Rooney asked, working quickly in the cold.

"Nothing that I can see," Faith replied, "but it's obvious to me that whoever came in here left in a hurry and was probably scared—and scarred—by my cat. Watson's amazingly territorial. He's like a watchdog that way. I'm guessing someone has a scratch or two this morning."

"Okay," the petite officer said, her dusting completed. "Let's go inside."

When they entered the kitchen, Officer Rooney stomped her feet and dropped her boots on a mat beside the door.

"Please have a seat in the living room," Faith offered. "I'll bring you a cup of coffee."

"Thank you. It's chilly out there."

A few minutes later, Faith walked into the living room with steaming mugs for herself and the officer.

Watson was sniffing at Officer Rooney's feet and trousers. Apparently satisfied, he settled back on his haunches but continued to survey her.

Harley screamed as though intent on making his presence known.

"What's this? A new addition?" the officer asked, placing her coffee on the table after a quick sample.

"This is Harley. He's Herbert Grissom's parrot."

"How'd you get stuck with him?"

"The bird was driving Mrs. Grissom crazy, so we offered to house him in the kennels. But later I brought him here for a while. I thought the parrot might reveal a clue or two about his master's death." Faith played with her mug and braced herself for a lecture about staying out of police business.

Officer Rooney raised her eyebrows and took up her coffee again. "Has he?"

"He repeats a few silly phrases. Nothing that makes much sense to me yet. But . . ." Faith took a deep breath, unsure whether she should even voice her crazy theory.

"What?" Officer Rooney inquired.

"The parrot may be what the intruder was after. I found a lot of stray feathers and signs of a struggle here in the living room. The couch pillows were tossed around, and my table nearby was knocked over. Watson usually isn't that destructive."

Officer Rooney went over to the bird's cage and paused at the small table near it. She picked up the square of chocolate Faith had left on it after finding it on the floor. "You weren't feeding this to him, were you?"

"No, I must have dropped it there. I'm a fan of chocolate. Midge told me not to give him chocolate or avocado because they're toxic for him."

"That's right. My parents owned a bird like this for several years." Officer Rooney took a notepad and a pen out of her pocket. "Do you think someone believes the parrot knows something about Mr. Grissom's murder? Someone besides you, that is?"

Faith swallowed. "Well, he says the normal parrot things like 'pretty boy,' but he also says things like 'more's the pity,' 'me hearty,' and 'turn over a new leaf.' Sometimes the phrases are jumbled up, which isn't unusual for birds that talk."

Officer Rooney made a note. "Do the words mean anything to you?"

"Kip Rudyard uses the phrase 'more's the pity,'" she said thoughtfully. "And we do know that Herbert was blackmailing him. So Harley may have picked that up from Kip. Chief Garris and Officer Laddy questioned him at length the other night. I can't believe he would try anything like this—not with so much suspicion already leveled against him."

"You'd be surprised what people will do when they feel backed into a corner. Any other phrases that jump out at you?"

"'Turn over a new leaf.' Herbert's wife told me her husband often said it, but she doesn't know why. He may have been planning to reform his ways—maybe to do right by the son he's never known."

"Turn over!" Harley shrieked. "Awk! Leaf! New leaf!"

"See what I mean about fractured phrases?" Faith asked.

Officer Rooney pursed her lips, studying the bird. "Yes, we've been filled in on Angelina Cordova's past marriage to Mr. Grissom. If she was willing to steal artwork and hide it, she might decide to steal the bird too."

"Angelina was with Brooke at the time," Faith said. "She was pretty upset. That's why Brooke stayed all night with her. She couldn't have been anywhere near my cottage."

Something in the back of her mind nagged at Faith. Could Angelina have gotten someone else to break into the cottage for her? Someone like Felix Anderson?

Faith had seen Felix and Angelina talking urgently together. He had been Herbert's partner, and maybe he knew Angelina too. Maybe they were in on it together. For all her impassioned explanations to the police, Angelina might—

"Let's wait and find out what the prints tell us, if anything," the officer said, interrupting Faith's thoughts. "We might only find your prints."

"I considered that."

"In the meantime, I suggest you keep this place locked up tight." Officer Rooney buttoned her jacket, thanked Faith for the coffee, and went in search of her boots. "Call us if anything else comes up." She gave Faith a knowing glance. "And don't wait seven or eight hours next time."

Faith watched Officer Rooney's car disappear, her mind whirling with questions about the odd break-in. Something drifted just out of her reach. Something to do with the forgotten square of chocolate she must have unwittingly dropped.

Suddenly she remembered Annie's comment about finding a chocolate wrapper behind the building. The kennel staffer had wondered if there were any kids at the retreat.

Was it possible that someone had been after Harley while he had been staying in the kennels? Did the person want to make the bird sick? Perhaps even kill him?

Or was she grasping at straws again?

Faith made sure Harley was fed and watered, then checked that all her doors and windows were secure.

She set out for the manor, Watson in tow. She was eager to see Brooke and find out how things had gone with Angelina during the night.

The morning had not lost its nighttime chill, despite a bright sun. The wind whipped snow into swirling drifts and tugged at her coat and scarf as she walked. She'd been hoping for a mild day—and especially a mild evening for the Christmas Walk in downtown Lighthouse Bay.

The merchants had been busy preparing for the big event. Their shops were already decorated with a plethora of colorful trimmings and lights. And tonight they would be offering special deals for shoppers and a large assortment of refreshments. There would be plenty of hot cider, sandwiches, chips, cookies, and various other holiday goodies. Midge was even planning special treats for the four-legged patrons who happened by.

The retreat guests would be attending the Christmas Walk, and Faith knew they were looking forward to the festivities. Maud planned to buy presents for everyone on her shopping list, Naomi was excited to see the lights, and Patsy couldn't wait to sample the refreshments.

When Faith and Watson entered the manor, the cat scampered off, most likely on the hunt for some feline adventure.

Faith made her way to the manor's basement and entered the kitchen, where Brooke was removing something that smelled delectable from the convection oven.

She was heartened by the sight of her friend. How wonderful it would be if this whole investigation were over, the perpetrator safely apprehended, and they could all get on with enjoying the season. But it seemed they were nowhere nearer to finding the answer.

"You're just the person I wanted to see," Brooke said, placing the baking sheet on the counter. "I need you to try one of these strawberry turnovers to see if they're edible."

Faith laughed. "It sounds like a tough job, but somebody has to do it."

Brooke set a pastry on a plate and handed it to Faith. "I'd better have one too." She served herself a turnover and poured two cups of coffee. They carried their pastries and coffee to the small table in the back corner and sat down.

Faith sampled the turnover immediately. "It's delicious."

Brooke took a bite of her pastry and chewed thoughtfully. "It could use a little more sugar."

"No, I like it this way," Faith protested. She glanced around the kitchen, then whispered, "Where's Angelina?"

"She's testing a turnover with Felix Anderson in the salon," Brooke answered, raising an eyebrow significantly.

"I saw them talking yesterday," Faith said. "I didn't realize they knew each other."

"They didn't until the retreat."

"How do you know?"

"Angelina mentioned Felix last night," Brooke said.

Faith leaned forward. "What did she say?"

"Apparently, Herbert told Felix that he had a son in Lighthouse Bay and he was here to find him. But Angelina didn't know that Herbert was searching for Kevin until she saw him at the welcome dinner."

"She was certainly shocked," Faith remarked.

"Yes." Brooke took a deep breath and let it out in a sigh. "She said Felix noticed her reaction to Herbert, and he put two and two together. He wishes he could have warned her about Herbert."

"Are you sure Angelina and Felix didn't know each other before the retreat?"

"The police wanted to know if there was a relationship between her and Felix too, but Angelina swears there wasn't. She says they've just gotten close quickly because they've bonded over being mistreated by Herbert."

"What do you think of them as murder suspects?" Faith took a sip of coffee.

"I know Angelina's not guilty of murder, and I don't think Felix is either."

"I hope you're right," Faith said, hearing the weariness in her own voice. "But someone is worried the truth will come out. Worried enough to break into my cottage and—"

"What?" Brooke nearly choked on her pastry. "When?"

"Last night. Wolfe walked me home after you and Angelina left. I didn't realize it at first, but then I saw that someone had jimmied the back door."

"Oh no! Are you and Watson okay?"

"We're fine, and nothing was missing."

"Did you call the police?" Brooke asked.

"I called them early this morning. Officer Rooney dusted for fingerprints, and we should know soon who they belong to—if there were any to be found besides my own."

"Are Watson and Harley all right?"

"They're both fine. In fact, I think the two of them scared off the intruder." Faith told her about the disordered living room and the flying feathers. "I believe Watson left his mark too—or marks. Did you happen to see any battle scars on Felix?"

"None that I noticed." Brooke wrapped her hands around her mug of steaming coffee. "This is getting scary. It must have something to do with Harley. Maybe you should get that bird out of your house."

"I can't say it doesn't make me nervous, but Harley seems to be the key to all this. Otherwise, why would someone be trying to get to him?"

"You need to be careful," Brooke cautioned.

Faith pushed back from the table and got up. "I should stop by the salon." She pointed to a tray of strawberry turnovers. "Do you want me to take some of these?"

"That would be great," Brooke replied. "Thanks."

In the salon, a smattering of guests had come in for early coffee before the day's schedule began. One of the guests was Maud. She was wheeling Mouse the Chihuahua in a sky-blue carrier.

The way Maud transported her pet like a baby in a stroller made Faith smile.

Maud caught Faith's eye and waved a piece of paper. "I'm so glad I found you!" she exclaimed, then reddened slightly, as if her boisterous greeting had drawn too much attention. Her eyes were lit with a conspiratorial gleam. "I have wonderful news."

"I can't wait to hear it," Faith said.

"Can we sit down for a minute?" Maud asked.

"Of course." Faith led Maud to a semi-secluded table and regarded the little dog. "It looks like Mouse is feeling chipper today. Is he eating better now?"

"He's right as rain, bless him." Maud draped her handbag over the carrier handle and scooted into a chair. "Thanks to you and Midge, who knew just what to do for him."

"I'm so glad," Faith said. "What did you want to tell me?"

Maud unfolded a legal-size document, smoothing its folds almost reverently, and set it down on the table. "You'll never guess."

"I think I can," Faith said, feeling the writer's contagious excitement. "You've landed a contract."

Maud smiled. "The marvelous Mr. Delacroix gave it to me yesterday, and I've been over the moon ever since."

Faith reached out to grasp the woman's hand. "That's fantastic. I'm so proud of you."

"Thank you! He said he just loves Bailey and offered me the contract to purchase both the story and the art. He wants it to be the launch publication for his new subsidiary in New York. Can you believe it?" Maud shook her springy gray curls, and her small jingle bell earrings tinkled. "It's the best Christmas present I could ever imagine."

"Congratulations," Faith said. "It's a delightful story."

"But I wonder if I could ask you a small favor," Maud said hesitantly.

"I'm new to this contract business. I told Mr. Delacroix that I'd like some time to review it. Would you mind taking a peek at it for me?"

"I'm not a literary agent or an attorney," Faith said, "and I haven't had much experience with contracts. Perhaps you should—"

"Please take a look at it for me," Maud pleaded. "I think you would be able to spot any inconsistencies or problems."

Faith couldn't disappoint her, so she relented. "I'm certainly willing to check it out, but I still think it would be best for you to contact someone more familiar with the way these things work."

Maud clapped. "You're wonderful and such a help to all of us. Thank you."

"I should be heading to the library," Faith said.

"You can take the contract with you and let me know tomorrow what you think." Maud folded the document and handed it to Faith. "I trust you. Thank you so much." She stood, then twirled Mouse's carrier about and sped away, humming.

Faith sighed. She tucked the contract carefully inside her large shoulder bag and left the room. She headed for the library, wondering when she could expect a call from Officer Rooney about the fingerprints.

Turning the corner at the end of the hall, she nearly collided with Kip. "Oh, I'm sorry," she breathed, wobbling slightly.

The part in Kip's hair was crooked, as though he'd gotten ready for the day quickly. A striped cardigan strained across his barrel chest. Surprise flitted across his face. "Well, if it isn't Marian the librarian. I didn't see you coming."

The appellation irritated her, even though she liked *The Music Man*. Somehow Kip always managed to rile her. This time she wouldn't correct him and offer her real name.

She gazed squarely into his pale eyes beneath heavy red brows. "I trust you enjoyed yesterday's festivities and are ready for a new day." She subtly studied his face and neck for evidence of Watson's handiwork, but she found none.

He wrinkled his nose as if he smelled something unpleasant. "There hasn't been much festiveness about this whole week with police popping up all over the place and asking their nagging questions. More's the pity."

Faith tightened her jaw. A man had been murdered, and Kip was complaining about the police asking questions. How could someone be so heartless, even if the victim had been blackmailing him? "Perhaps if everyone minded their own business and behaved like good citizens, the police presence wouldn't be necessary." Without waiting for a response, she breezed past him.

She heard only a snort as she hurried away.

A few minutes later, Faith entered the library and sat down at her desk. She took a deep breath and realized that for the first time she was looking forward to the end of this retreat.

Faith loved her job. She enjoyed meeting new people and helping to organize special literary conferences and retreats for booklovers. Yesterday afternoon's Christmas party for the children had been inspiring and fun, but Herbert's murder and everything she'd discovered since then had severely dampened her enthusiasm.

She extracted Maud's contract from her shoulder bag and spread it out on the desk. At least here was a bright spot. Maud's story was going to be published. A dream was coming true for a kind and talented woman.

She waded through the official language, trying to make sense of the literary legalese. The document listed the advance payment and the agreement relating to royalties. To Faith, it all seemed standard and acceptable.

Maple Publishing of Quebec, Canada, has the right to reproduce, distribute, or authorize . . . the Work in all formats. This includes primary rights as well as subsidiary rights . . . Author agrees not to publish, sell, license, or offer for publication, sale, or license any Competing Work without written agreement in advance . . .

On and on. But suddenly she stopped and stared at the name of the new subsidiary company.

New Leaf Publishing.

18

New Leaf. Thoughts whirled through Faith's head with incredible speed. Was it possible?

The parrot's grating voice echoed through her mental maelstrom. *New leaf. Turn over! New leaf. Awk!*

Could Herbert have been speaking of something quite different than she had previously assumed? Maybe he hadn't been talking about his son or his wife. Katrina had said that Herbert boasted about "turning over a new leaf" and claimed it would make them rich. Forging a relationship with his estranged son would hardly result in riches.

Had the phrase referred to something altogether different? Perhaps an alliance with a well-regarded company that would publish his work?

But Leo had denied knowing Herbert. Even though Faith had been a little surprised when Leo had called him Herbie, he could have easily overheard the nickname as he claimed.

Faith opened her laptop and searched for Maple Publishing in Quebec.

As she skimmed their website, she noticed their mission statement was prominently displayed. *We are committed to partnering with exceptional artists from all over the world to create the highest quality books for children.*

Then she delved into the publisher's history. The company had been founded in the late eighteenth century and had a prestigious record for a family-owned business that had become prosperous and esteemed for its quality and production.

Through the years, the publisher had gone through seemingly normal ups and downs. They were probably related to political upheavals and economic variances.

Faith found a somewhat cryptic reference to Reginald Martin, a former president and CEO who had experienced an unusually difficult downturn that had nearly brought the company to ruin. Plagued by ill health, Reginald had been forced to retire. But in the ten years following the near disaster, Maple Publishing had rallied and reclaimed its competitive edge.

Léon Delacroix was listed as acquisitions director for children's books. She searched the site for other mentions of him but found none. She wished she knew someone connected with Maple Publishing who might know some personal history about the man.

Faith was so engrossed in the colorful website that she didn't immediately notice someone had approached. She glanced up to find Patsy standing close to her desk. Had she been snooping over Faith's shoulder?

"Excuse me," Patsy said. "I'm sorry to disturb you, but I would love to see that spectacular 1912 edition of ''Twas the Night Before Christmas' again."

"Of course," Faith answered. "Right this way." She got up from her desk and went to procure the book and gloves.

When Patsy was set up with the book at the table, Faith scanned the library. Several other guests were searching for resources, so she went to assist them. It was proving to be a busy morning. She would have to postpone further computer searches.

During a lull, Katrina walked into the library. She was accompanied by a woman who appeared slightly older than she was. There was a striking resemblance between the women, and Faith assumed they were related.

Faith was surprised to see Katrina, who had mainly stayed out of sight after the fiasco with Kip. Perhaps her companion had bolstered her confidence to the degree that she was willing to leave her room and mingle with the other guests.

She greeted Katrina and the other woman with her brightest smile. "It's good to see you."

"This is Faith Newberry," Katrina said stiffly. "She's the librarian here. Faith, this is Helga Metzger. She is my sister from Bonn, Germany. She has come to stay with me."

Helga smiled at Faith. There was a warm crinkling around her blue eyes. "I am pleased to meet you," she said with perfect elocution and a pleasant accent. "I have been admiring this beautiful library. I told Katrina I had to see it."

"Allow me to give you a tour." Faith fell into step with the pair and pointed out various features of the library and related how the mansion had been in the Jaxon family for over a century. "Mrs. Jaxon had the idea to turn the manor into a literary retreat several years ago, and it's been a very productive use of their ancestral home."

They chatted amiably, stopping to admire the marble fireplace, the rare books in glass cases, the magnificent Christmas tree. But at the back of Faith's mind was the idea that Herbert might have had some connection with New Leaf Publishing. She wondered if Katrina would be able to tell her more about New Leaf.

After giving them the tour, Faith returned to her desk while the women perused the bookcases.

The library door opened, and Faith's occasional helper, Laura, came in. "I finished my duties early, so Ms. Russell said I could come help you in here if you need it."

"Actually, your timing is perfect," Faith said, thinking fast. "Could you watch the library for me for a while?"

Laura grinned. "I'd be happy to."

"We have a new guest, Ms. Metzger, who is Mrs. Grissom's sister from Germany. I was going to ask the two of them to have coffee with me to ensure they feel welcome." *And hopefully to find out whether Katrina knows anything about New Leaf Publishing.*

"I'm glad Mrs. Grissom's sister is here," Laura said. "She must be grateful to have family with her during such a hard time."

"I'm sure she is. Thank you for taking over." Faith went over to

Katrina and Helga. "There's coffee in the salon. Would you like to join me?"

Katrina furrowed her brow. "I must—"

"We would love that," Helga broke in. "*Danke schön.* Thank you very much."

Faith led them to the salon. When they were seated, Faith poured coffee, offered pastries, and kept up a lighthearted conversation.

"What do you do in Bonn?" she asked Helga. She liked this older version of Katrina with the same fair hair drawn back and slightly streaked with gray.

Helga took a sip of coffee. "I am a professor at a university."

Faith reflected on the divergent lifestyles and fortunes of the two sisters as she told them about her former position as librarian and archivist at Hawarden University in Boston.

Eventually, the matter of Herbert's death injected itself as Faith had hoped it would.

Folding her well-groomed hands in her lap, Helga engaged Faith with a straightforward gaze. "How long do you think it might be before the body will be released and my sister can have some closure?"

Katrina lowered her head and fiddled with her napkin.

"I wish I knew," Faith responded carefully. "The police are still investigating. I know this is difficult."

"My sister is no killer," Helga said with a touch of steel in her voice.

Katrina faced her sister. "Say what you think. You believe I should have listened to you and not married Herbie."

"*Liebchen*—" Helga began, using a term of endearment.

"Please," Faith broke in, eager to deflect an argument between the sisters. "Nothing has been decided yet, and there are other people with motives. But the truth has a way of coming out."

The three women sat in silence for a moment.

Faith picked up the carafe, poured more coffee into their cups, then turned to Katrina. "Is there anything else you can tell me about why your husband came to this retreat?"

Katrina sighed. "I said before that Herbie did not tell me his plans. He was like that. He just decided something and off we went. But he thought something good will happen. You know, he was always talking about turning over a new leaf."

"What do you mean by that?" Faith persisted. "Did he ever talk about a subsidiary company called New Leaf Publishing?"

Katrina shrugged. "I don't remember. He said he must see someone here and show them his pictures to make us rich. And then someone took them."

"Who?" Faith urged, feeling her heart start to pound. "Who did he want to see here?"

"I don't know. I told the police that. I am tired." Katrina glanced at Helga. "I want to go now."

"Please tell me who," Faith pleaded. "It could be so important to bringing this all to a close."

"People are coming," Katrina said, motioning to the door. "Too many people. I need to leave."

Faith glanced over and saw several guests entering the salon. She knew there would be no more talking to Katrina now.

"*Danke* for your kindness," Helga told Faith. Then she took her sister's arm and guided her out of the room.

With a sigh, Faith retraced her steps to the library. She nearly collided with Leo in the doorway.

He appeared purposeful, almost stern. He glanced at her, then at his watch. When Leo looked at her again, his features had softened. "I was hoping to see you before I left for my appointment."

"Is there something I can help you with?"

"No. I must go so I can get back in time for this evening's downtown event." Leo gave her a small bow and rushed down the hallway.

He had been polite but not nearly as attentive as he usually was.

Maybe he was finally getting the message that she was not bowled over by his charm and good looks. So why did she feel a little sad? Was it a wounded ego?

When Faith entered the library, she noticed Wolfe talking to Howard Watkins and another guest near the fireplace.

Faith smiled to see Watson weaving around Wolfe's ankles. Wolfe bent to give the cat a quick pat before rising and continuing his conversation.

"How did your coffee break go?" Laura asked.

"It was fine," Faith replied. "I'm sorry I was out a bit longer than I expected."

"No problem. But I'd better get going now." Laura strode out the door before Faith could thank her again.

Faith returned to her desk and wiggled the mouse to awaken her computer. The website for Maple Publishing sprang to life. She chided herself for not closing the page before she left.

Glancing down, she saw she'd left Maud's contract there too. She paused. She was almost sure she had left it on the right, near her pencil caddy. Now it was on the left. Had Patsy taken a peek while Faith was having coffee with the two sisters?

She felt troubled. She should have known better than to leave Maud's contract out on her desk where someone could see it.

"Good morning."

Startled, she found Wolfe standing at her desk. The two men were gone, but Watson had trotted after him and now stared at both humans, clearly demanding further attention. "I'm sorry. I didn't realize you were done with your conversation."

"The two gentlemen had a few questions about the rare books section, and I was able to help them."

"Good," she said.

"Are you planning to go to the Christmas Walk tonight?"

Faith nodded. "It's generated a lot of excitement among the guests. I think everyone is going."

"I'm glad I'll be able to get away. I think it's important to show my support for the shop owners of our fair town. I was wondering if you would care to accompany me."

She tried to ignore a silly uptick in her pulse. "Yes, I'd be glad to."

Wolfe smiled. "I'll pick you up at your place at five. Will that work?"

"I'll be ready."

He smiled at her and left.

Faith snuggled Watson on her lap. She mentally searched her closet for something suitable to wear tonight.

Her cell phone sounded, jarring her.

It was Eileen. "How are you, honey?"

"Just fine," Faith answered. "I've been busy, and my house was broken into last night—"

"What?" Eileen squawked. "Are you hurt?"

"I'm all right," Faith reassured her. "Whoever it was didn't even take anything. I think Watson scared off the intruder. Officer Rooney came out and dusted for prints this morning." In an effort to distract her aunt, she added, "Wolfe just asked if I'd go to the Christmas Walk with him."

It worked like a charm. "Ah, I see," Eileen said knowingly.

"See what?" Faith asked innocently. "Everyone will be there. It's not a date or anything. He simply—"

"Of course it's a date. And I couldn't be happier. He's a good man, and it's plain as day he's taken with you. It's about time he got around to doing something about it."

Faith laughed. "You're impossible, but I love you anyway."

"Have you heard anything new regarding the investigation?" Eileen asked quietly. "Do you think the break-in was related?"

"I don't know yet, but I've been keeping my eyes and ears open. Harley says phrases that sound like nonsense most of the time, but lately I've been wondering if there might be a connection between Herbert and a new subsidiary of Maple Publishing called New Leaf."

Eileen was silent for a long moment.

"Are you still there?" Faith asked.

"I'm here. Listen, the reason I called is that I've been researching that fancy publisher of yours from Canada."

"And?" Faith urged.

"Well, I haven't learned anything definitive," Eileen said, "but I discovered something interesting. A few years ago, he officially changed his last name from Martin to Delacroix."

"How did you find out?"

"Through his military record. He probably didn't think the name Martin was sophisticated enough." Eileen gave a derisive snort. "In any case, it's something the police should know."

Something nagged at the back of Faith's mind. "It's odd, but sometimes people change their name for legitimate reasons."

"True," Eileen admitted. "What do the attendees think of him?"

"He's been very popular," Faith replied drily, "especially with the women. He has chosen Maud Tompkins's story about the Bastille mouse to launch the publisher's American children's line."

"I'm thrilled for her. *Bailey the Bastille Mouse* was the best part of the story reading segment of the Christmas party. Which, by the way, was a splendid success."

"I'm so glad the kids enjoyed it."

"Oh, I've got to go. There's a line at my desk. I'll see you tonight." Eileen clicked off.

Faith held the cell phone to her ear for a moment, the name Martin sticking in her mind. Where had she heard it?

And then she remembered. She returned to the website for Maple Publishing. She found the history section and scanned it.

There it was: Reginald Martin, the president and CEO under whose watch the company had nearly been brought to ruin. Reginald had been the son of Nicholas Martin, the publishing mogul credited with the company's early success. Reginald had retired nine years ago. It was after the company nearly went under. He was replaced by someone named Carstairs, the current president.

It could be a coincidence. Martin was a common name. Yet Delacroix held a position in that same publishing company.

She read through it again. Was it possible Léon Delacroix was the son of Reginald Martin? Had he changed his name to distance himself from a company failure?

Faith powered down her computer, too antsy to sit still any longer. Besides, the guests were gone, and the library was empty.

Without fully framing her intentions, Faith went in search of Marlene, with Watson at her heels, and found the assistant manager in her basement office.

Marlene was elbow deep in papers, and she appeared more than a little disgruntled when she glimpsed Faith and Watson in the doorway. "Is there something you need?" she demanded, her tone decidedly icy.

"Mr. Delacroix asked me to drop off a folder to his room," she said, patting her shoulder bag as if it held such a folder. "I need to leave in a little while and thought it best to put it inside his door. It's a bit too large to slip underneath. Would it be all right if I borrow the key to the Mark Twain Suite?"

Marlene gave her a look somewhere between envy and irritation. Her interest in Leo had not been returned, and yet here was the librarian, chummy enough to have earned the man's attention.

"I promise I'll bring the key right back," Faith added.

"See that *he* doesn't get in there." Marlene glowered at Watson. "You know the rule about pets in the guests' rooms—that is, pets not belonging to the guest—and Mr. Delacroix had the good sense not to bring an animal." She waved a hand at her key ring on the desk and once again bent over her paperwork.

"Thank you." Faith snagged the key ring, then picked up Watson and left.

What am I thinking? She wrestled with her conscience as she made her way upstairs to the guest suites.

Leo had left less than an hour ago, and he had indicated that he worried about returning in time for the evening's Christmas Walk, so surely he wasn't back yet. She could take a peek inside his room and get out before anyone was the wiser.

But what would she be searching for?

Maybe she would know when she saw it.

She all but snorted at the idea, yet she kept walking.

When she reached the second floor, she was relieved to find it deserted. Even so, she was glad for her low-heeled, soft-soled shoes as she crept down the corridor.

Ignoring the cautioning voice in her head, she unlocked the door to the Mark Twain Suite. She held Watson firmly as she went inside, then closed the door with infinite care.

The cat squirmed in her arms, so she let him down to explore the unfamiliar surroundings. Marlene had ordered her not to take him inside, but more than once in the past, Watson had found something she would have missed.

Faith stood in the spacious suite, which was impeccably detailed and orderly, and glanced around.

The coffee table near the leather sofa was bare except for a folded edition of the *Lighthouse Bay Observer*. The bed with its brown-and-gold coverlet had been made with military precision. In the closet, suitcases were lined up neatly side by side, and a single suit in a garment bag hung from the shiny pole.

Though the conference wasn't scheduled to end until tomorrow night's farewell banquet, it appeared Leo was packed up and ready to go.

When she turned, she saw that Watson had leaped onto the bed and was pawing at something stuck between the bed and the dresser.

Faith went to investigate and spotted a bit of tan leather. She rescued it from her inquisitive feline. It resembled an oversize wallet—something that might fit inside the deep inner pocket of a suit jacket.

Against the voice of her conscience, she opened the leather wallet.

It held a single newspaper clipping from the *Quebec Chronicle-Telegraph* dated five years earlier. Below the masthead a headline read, *Publishing Mogul's Death Ruled Probable Suicide.*

Faith's heart hammered in her chest so loudly she was sure it could be heard in neighboring suites.

The photo beneath the headline showed a silver-haired man in his midsixties and a woman with very dark hair and eyes. The caption read, *Reginald Martin with wife, Celeste Martin, née Delacroix.*

She skimmed the article and gathered that the man had died when he wrapped his car around a tree. It related a brief account of his retirement from Maple Publishing following a "long battle over a libel suit." Surviving relatives included Joanne Martin Smythe and Léon Albert Martin.

How long she stood stunned and unable to move, Faith didn't know. When her head stopped spinning, she slipped the clipping back into the leather folder and tucked it between the bed and the dresser where she'd found it.

She scooped up Watson and fled from the Mark Twain Suite, the hot breath of some invisible doom following her.

19

Late-afternoon sunlight slanted across the landscape, deepening its shadows as Faith ran outside. It felt good to be out in the open—out of the suite she'd had no business entering.

The secrets that were buried in another's life should remain his provenance alone. Shouldn't they? How awful that Reginald Martin had taken his own life five years after he had been forced to retire.

She suddenly remembered a conversation with Leo on the coach traveling to the theater for the Christmas musical.

A frighteningly otherworldly look had altered his features when he asked if she had ever lost someone dear to her. She recalled his words: *But when it grabs you by the throat, you never quite throw off its ugly hand. It clings to you, and it tightens around you until—* Then he had slumped into a deep silence for a while before recovering his usual banter.

Had Leo been referring to his father and mother? They had to be the people in the newspaper clipping. Leo looked too much like both of them for any other explanation to make sense. *Suicide. Wrapped his car around a tree.*

She wished she could have studied the clipping more, but fear had made her hurry—a fear that drove her to dash home with Watson snug in her arms.

Why would Leo carry a five-year-old news story in a leather binder rather than leave it at home in a desk drawer or an album?

But what did it have to do with Herbert? The phrase *new leaf* repeated in her head over and over. And Katrina's report that Herbert believed "turning over a new leaf" would involve money.

Night was beginning to fall across the snow-covered terrain. She had to get ready to accompany Wolfe to the Christmas Walk. Eileen, Brooke, and Midge would also be there, and she looked forward to seeing them.

Still breathing hard from nervousness and exertion, she pulled her key from her jacket pocket and thrust it into the lock. She was glad for the safety of home.

Suddenly, Watson lurched from her arms, back arched, fur standing on end, hissing.

At the same instant, someone rounded the corner of her cottage.

It was Leo. What a shock to see him when she had only just come from sneaking into his room. Could he have known somehow? *No, that's ridiculous.* "What are you doing here?" she blurted out.

"Do forgive me." Leo lowered his head in a half bow and shivered in his suit jacket. He wore no overcoat, only a woolen scarf that flapped over his shoulders in the rising wind. "I didn't realize when I went out for a walk that the temperature had dropped to such a level. I'm quite chilled. Would it be all right if I came inside to warm up?"

"Well, I—" Faith hedged.

"Just for a few minutes. That is, if it's no trouble." He smiled ingratiatingly. "Then I'll make my way back to the manor."

She was startled to hear a low growl from Watson. The cat had shown his dislike of Leo the first time they met, but she hadn't thought too much about it. Now she wondered what she might be missing and if there was a good reason to be wary. "I am in something of a hurry."

"I promise I won't keep you long," Leo said, shivering.

"It is awfully cold," she said. "You should have worn a hat in this weather." *I sound like my mother*, she thought.

"I'm so sorry to be a bother, but there is something I wanted to say . . ." His voice trailed off, and there was desperate pleading in his expression.

"Please come in," Faith said as she opened the door.

Watson raced past them into the cottage.

Faith and Leo followed the cat inside.

Faith shrugged out of her fleece jacket, wondering what he wanted to talk to her about and trying to ignore her nerves. She ushered him into the living room. "Have a seat."

Harley shrieked from his cage near the window.

"Hello, Harley," she said and unlatched his cage door so he could use the perch on top of the cage.

The bird had been cooped up all day, but he only stared at her now without moving.

"A handsome fellow," Leo remarked. His cheeks and nose were red from the cold, and his usually perfect silver hair was windblown. He sat tentatively on a chair and rubbed his hands together, probably to warm them, but he appeared unsettled, unlike his usual put-together self.

Watson hopped onto the couch near Harley's cage, ears erect, perhaps daring the bird to come out.

The two seemed to have become friends the night before, and Faith had to smile as she bustled about the kitchen. She poured two mugs of hot chocolate and put a couple of scones on a plate.

When she brought the refreshments into the living room, Leo was sitting with his head bent and his hands clasped between his knees. He didn't say a word. He simply stared at the small tray she set before him.

This was not the Léon Delacroix she knew. What had happened? "Have some cocoa," she said. "It will warm you."

"Awk! New leaf. Turn over!" the parrot chanted into the silence.

Still Leo did not move toward the cocoa or lift his head.

Faith sat down across from him and cradled her cup in her hands.

It seemed hours rather than minutes before he finally raised his head. And in that movement, the woolen scarf slipped low on his neck.

With a shock, she noticed two angry red streaks. It had been Leo in her cottage, Leo whom Watson had attacked. Blood rushed to her head. The urge to flee seized her.

He stared directly at her. The redness from the wind and cold was gone, and in the ashen pallor of his face his eyes burned like coals. "You know, don't you?" he said in a low voice.

She waited, the sense of dread deepening. "Know what?"

"Playing dumb doesn't suit you." Leo glanced in the direction of Harley's cage, peering into some distance beyond it. "He's the reason I came here."

Faith felt her stomach tighten. "Mr. Grissom?" she asked in a small voice.

"No need to pretend. You've been prying into my life. You know." He spoke in a dull tone that made Faith's heart constrict. "You know about me. And about my father."

Faith averted her eyes. "I'm sorry about your father," she whispered.

His mouth twisted downward, and his chin trembled. "I wanted Grissom to know. I wanted him to see what he did."

Faith was afraid to speak, afraid to break the spell he seemed to be under. She didn't move a muscle.

"He destroyed my father's career, left him sick at heart, which in some ways is worse than being sick in body." Leo clenched his fists. "Five years ago, on December 15, my father never came home."

December 15. The same date she'd found Herbert Grissom dead in the snow at Castleton Manor.

Faith couldn't speak. Surreptitiously, she reached for her cell phone where it burned against her hip. She must let someone know she was in trouble.

"Don't do that," Leo said, rising. He lurched toward her. "Please don't do that," he repeated, almost begging.

She cringed.

"I'll take your phone, *s'il vous plaît*," he added.

Faith had no choice. She gave him her phone.

"Thank you," he said courteously. He pocketed her phone and returned to the chair. He sat down again and put both hands to his temples.

She checked the wall clock. If Wolfe was on time, he'd be calling for her in thirty minutes. *Please be on time. Or better yet, come early.*

"I wanted Grissom to see what he did, what his lawsuit had accomplished." Leo gave a mirthless little laugh.

"What did he do?" Faith asked, trying to stall for time.

"My father made an honest mistake by attributing commissioned artwork to another artist, but Grissom claimed it had done irreparable damage to his career." Leo grimaced. "He bilked Maple Publishing and my father out of a fortune."

Faith leaned forward, her heart hammering. She recalled the large payment Herbert had obtained for artwork through an agent the police had been unable to locate. The money had been funneled into an offshore account. Had Herbert received the money from Leo's father?

"I brought the newspaper clipping all the way from Quebec. I showed it to Grissom out there by the fountain in the snow." His eyelashes fluttered, as though he were seeing it all again.

"You killed him," Faith whispered.

Leo drew a long breath, then peered at her as though suddenly realizing she was there. His eyes grew wide and pleading. "I didn't mean to. I only wanted him to know what he'd done. But he laughed at me and said, 'Hard times come to us all, me hearty.'"

"Me hearty!" Harley shrieked. "Me hearty! Awk!"

The sound made them both jump.

A moment later, silence descended.

Faith glanced over Leo's shoulder. Darkness was falling fast. Was that a light beyond the trees? Could it be Wolfe? Or the police watching, as the chief had said?

Look away, she told herself. *Don't let him see.* She clenched her teeth to keep from trembling.

Leo's dull voice resumed. "I reached into my pocket for the clipping, but then . . ." His black eyes began to flame, like coals stirred by a poker. "He pulled the cutlass from his belt and waved it in my face. I grabbed it, and we struggled. I kept slipping on the ice. And then he fell." A veil came over his eyes, and his voice dropped to a whisper. "The cutlass . . ." He shuddered. "I told him to get up, but he didn't move."

"You could have gone for help," Faith said, finding her voice. "But you left him there to die."

His lips twisted, then stilled. "It was only right," he said as if trying to convince himself as much as her. "The fates decreed it."

"It wasn't right," she said, surprised at her boldness. "You chose to do what you did. You also chose to let the others—Katrina, Kip, and Angelina—take the blame."

Harley shrieked again, piercing the charged atmosphere.

"And you also chose to break in here," Faith continued. "I found the chocolate and the wrapper you dropped at the kennels when you were trying to poison that poor bird."

"Well, Miss Newberry," Leo said, giving her a chilling smile, "you seem to have all the answers. But the question now is, what is to be done with you?"

"No, the question is, will you tell the truth?" she replied, trying to sound firm instead of terrified. "You said you didn't mean to do it. You could explain—"

"But who will believe me?" he interrupted. "Especially when they find out, as they surely will, that I arranged to meet Grissom here, that I told him I would purchase his work for New Leaf Publishing. I told him he must tell no one or the deal was off. So you see, I can't do what you suggest. And I can't let you speak to the police either."

Faith could hardly breathe.

He drummed his fingers on the armrest of the chair, then seemed to come to a decision. "That's why you're coming with me."

She straightened. "That's crazy. Someone will see us."

Leo stood, covered the distance between them in a few quick steps, and seized her arms. His hands burned into her flesh, and his face was close enough that she could feel his breath. "You must do exactly as I say. Please don't make me do something we'll both regret."

Though he'd brandished no gun, his meaning was clear. She felt the menace of his words, the pain in her arms as he gripped her harder. "Please don't do this. It will only make it worse. You have to—"

"Quiet!" he snapped, raising his voice for the first time. "We're going out the back door. My car is only a few yards away. It's parked beneath the trees. No one will see."

Was he mad? Did he really think he could whisk her away in his car—perhaps all the way across the border into Canada? "I'm not going anywhere with you."

Leo pinned her arms behind her back and whirled her around toward the back door. "I don't want to hurt you, but you're coming with me."

She stumbled, nearly falling as he pushed her forward into the kitchen.

And then suddenly, all chaos broke loose. Watson leaped from the refrigerator onto Leo's head, raking his claws across the man's face and neck. At the same time, Harley flew out of his cage and straight at Leo with a horrendous screech, powerful wings beating at the man. The bird screamed loud enough to wake the dead.

Leo released Faith's arms and attempted to fend off his attackers, howling.

The back door burst open to reveal Chief Garris and Wolfe. Garris leveled his weapon at Leo and ordered, "Give it up, Delacroix. You're under arrest for killing Herbert Grissom."

Watson and Harley backed off, and Garris cuffed Leo while reading him his rights.

Wolfe came and helped Faith to a chair just in time before her knees buckled. "Are you all right?"

"I am now," she said. Watson jumped into her lap, purring. "Thanks to you and this guy."

"This was the most beautiful Christmas Walk I've ever seen," Maud announced as she cuddled her little dog, Mouse.

Faith had missed most of the event but for a final candle-lit procession. After spending a couple of hours at the police station, she had returned to the cottage to check on Watson and Harley. The pair had once again been sitting companionably when she walked in, neither one the worse for wear.

Now Faith and Watson sat in the salon at the manor with Wolfe, Eileen, Brooke, Midge, and Marlene. A few of the retreat guests, including Maud, Patsy, and Howard, had also joined the party. Brooke set out sugar cookies, spiced cider, and hot chocolate, and Christmas music played softly in the background.

"It's hard to believe that Mr. Delacroix chose this retreat to take revenge on poor Mr. Grissom," Patsy remarked.

"Not so poor," Maud said quietly, absently tracing the rim of her cup. "He was a pirate in real life. His greed nearly brought disaster on Maple Publishing. It did bring disaster on Reginald Martin."

Faith regarded her fondly. Maud had placed strong hopes on her contract with Maple's subsidiary, New Leaf, and she might well have worried about the fate of her contract. The company would most likely honor it, for Leo had acted on their behalf as acquisitions editor.

But Faith knew if it didn't work out with New Leaf Publishing, other publishers would soon express interest in Maud's spectacular work. *Bailey the Bastille Mouse* was sure to become a favorite book of children all over the world.

"It's all very sad," Howard commented. His faithful labradoodle lay at his feet, occasionally availing himself of the crumbs his master dropped. "I mean, imagine carrying a grudge for so many years."

"Did Katrina know about Leo's resentment against her husband?" Eileen asked.

"The chief said Leo threatened her," Faith responded. "But she didn't know anything about Leo or his father until now."

"Leo's anger put a lot of people in jeopardy, including Faith," Midge said. She sat on Faith's left and rested a hand on her friend's arm. "She might have been spirited away to Canada and who knows what fate if it hadn't been for the intervention of Watson and Harley."

Watson, curled up on Faith's lap, looked smug and leaned into the ear rub Faith offered.

"Watson and Harley were marvelous," Faith agreed. "But the credit really goes to Wolfe, whose suspicion led the police to investigate Leo's alibi." She flushed a little. *Did I really think he disliked Leo out of jealousy?*

"What did they find?" Brooke asked.

"Traffic cameras caught him in Lighthouse Bay a full twenty-four hours ahead of his stated arrival time," Wolfe explained.

"When the police put it together with what Eileen told them about the name change," Faith said, "it really heated things up."

"Marlene deserves kudos too," Wolfe said. "When she told me that Faith hadn't returned the key to the Mark Twain Suite like she promised, we knew something had gone wrong."

Marlene blushed but uncharacteristically said nothing. She seemed subdued after she'd heard about the arrest of Léon Delacroix.

"So, how's Katrina holding up?" Brooke asked.

"I saw her earlier, and she seems to be doing all right under the circumstances," Marlene replied. "She's flying to Germany with her sister as soon as they take care of the arrangements."

Faith hoped the widow would be able to come to terms with her husband's death and find peace in her home country.

"What about Harley?" Eileen asked, then turned to Faith. "I don't suppose you've decided to keep him."

Faith smiled. "Although Watson and Harley made a great team, I don't think Watson would ever forgive me if we kept the parrot."

Watson rubbed his head against her hand and purred.

"Annie Jennings told me she'd like to adopt him," Marlene said.

Midge grinned. "What great news."

The door opened, and Felix burst through with a laughing Angelina and Kevin. They waved at the group and made a beeline for the refreshments.

Faith turned to Wolfe. "At least something good has come out of all this," she whispered as she gestured toward the three latecomers.

Angelina deserved some happiness after all she'd been through. Felix had found something too—friendship and ... Well, who knew? Maybe the three of them together would share the love and joy that Christmas was all about.

"I'm glad it's over and you're safe," Wolfe told Faith in a low voice.

The look he gave her warmed her like sunshine. Faith had an overwhelming sense of well-being, surrounded by dear friends who watched out for her.

She hugged her precious cat closer as a strain of her favorite carol echoed in her heart.

I heard the bells on Christmas Day,
Their old, familiar carols play,
And wild and sweet the words repeat
Of peace on earth, goodwill to men.